Truce – A War Saga

TRUCE

A War Saga

T. STYLES

By T. Styles

ARE YOU ON OUR EMAIL LIST?

SIGN UP ON OUR WEBSITE

www.thecartelpublications.com

OR TEXT THE WORD: CARTELBOOKS TO

22828

FOR PRIZES, CONTESTS, ETC.

Check Out Other Titles By The Cartel Publications

By T. Styles

Truce – A War Saga   5

WWW.THECARTELPUBLICATIONS.COM

By T. Styles

TRUCE – A WAR SAGA

SAGA

By

T. STYLES

ISBN 10: 1948373157

ISBN 13: 978-1948373159

Cover Design: Book Slut Girl

First Edition
Printed in the United States of America

By T. Styles

WAR
Series
in Order

War

War 2: All Hell Breaks Loose

War 3: Land of The Lou's

War 4: Skull Island

War 5: Karma

War 6: Envy

War 7: Pink Cotton

Truce: A War Saga

What Up Fam,

First off, I pray that ya'll are doing well and are not too overwhelmed. Since I last wrote a note to you, there have been several tragedies that have taken place. Murders of black men and women are happening in this country as if it's a sport. Protect yourselves at all costs. Not just physically, but mentally as well. Change will come and we will be better for it. Just hold on and do what you can to make a difference. Starting with voting. If you're not registered to vote, please go to: https://www.voteamerica.com/register-to-vote/ today and show up on Tuesday, November 3, 2020. It's imperative!

Now, onto the book in hand... *TRUCE*. Mannnnn, T. did it again! The humor this woman possesses is mind boggling to me. While reading this novel I had quite a few loud outbursts of laughs! And...I have a new FAVORITE character. I'm not going to mention who it is because I don't wanna bias you guys, but I believe you'll be able to guess. I'm sure ya'll gonna love this person too! *TRUCE* is an amazing story and another instant classic!

By T. Styles

With that being said, keeping in line with tradition, we want to give respect to a vet or new trailblazer paving the way. In this novel, we would like to recognize:

BREONNA TAYLOR
AHMAUD ARBERY
GEORGE FLOYD
and
RAYSHARD BROOKS

God bless these soul's families and all the families of the lives we've lost as well as our nation. Please do not let them have died in vain. Amen.

Aight Fam, I love ya'll and will talk to you again soon!

God Bless!

Charisse "C. Wash" Washington

Vice President

The Cartel Publications

www.thecartelpublications.com

www.facebook.com/publishercwash

Instagram: publishercwash

www.twitter.com/cartelbooks

www.facebook.com/cartelpublications

Follow us on Instagram: Cartelpublications

#CartelPublications

#UrbanFiction

#PrayForCece

#RIPBreonnaTaylor

#RIPAhmaudArbery

#RIPGeorgeFloyd

#RIPRayshardBrooks

#BLM

#Truce

PROLOGUE

A celebration was underway...

As waiters dressed in black and white littered the spectacular hall, holding gold trays with hors d'oeuvres and champagne flutes, it was obvious that in the midst of the crowd was a star. And she just so happened to be the hostess. The excitement was in the way that every invitee looked upon her face. It was in the way they laughed at her jokes.

More than all, it was in the mystery surrounding her presence.

For you see, Blaire Petit was a strange beautiful woman who to some, seemed to appear from nowhere, only to claim her position at her wealthy grandmother's side. Up until two years ago, no one knew Gina even had a granddaughter, let alone one of African American descent.

The reason was simple. Gina was estranged from her daughter, who ran away due to her mother's controlling, evil and possessive ways. And she was up to her old tricks at present.

By T. Styles

It was accurate as fuck, that Blair had a full life until it was stolen by the grandmother who years before, Blaire didn't know existed.

Born Blakeslee Wales in the 70's, she always knew she was different than most girls. Her walk had a slight bop to it that was more fitting of a prince than a princess. Upon first glance during the younger years, gossipers would whisper that she was gay, but Blakeslee's spirit reasoned her dismay reached deeper.

She didn't want to be 'like a boy'.

She wanted to be a boy.

Many years and many moons later, this little girl changed her gender and became Banks Wales, a dangerous drug kingpin and family man. A millionaire many times over, he fashioned his luxurious lifestyle in the way he always desired as a child. Complete with a wife, Bethany Wales, who, via vitro fertilization, bore him four children. One from his direct bloodline. Although the marriage didn't end well due to her infidelity and his disgust with her weak personality, he still took care of her financially until she was murdered.

But life goes on, right?

So, without missing a beat, he entered a second relationship and this arrangement was definitely *taboo, as his new woman was also his best friend's wife. She also bore him children. Twin boys, Ace and Walid, along with a little girl whom he never met name Blakeslee Wales. All via Banks' eggs which he had frozen in the event he wanted more biological children.*

And then something horrific happened.

After suffering severe headaches, Banks received a botched brain surgery to have a tumor removed, which was dangerously close to taking his life. Fortunately, and unfortunately at the same time, Gina, who he never knew was related, gained news about the surgery and arranged to have him brought to her mansion like a thief in the night.

Upon hiring a team of the best doctors, his life was saved. Still, there was a long road to recovery, as Banks would need to learn everything from scratch. How to walk. And how to talk. Gina used this time to teach him the haircare and skincare business, and she was shocked at how easily Banks sucked up the knowledge.

But to those who knew him, it all made sense, because you couldn't build a multimillion-dollar drug operation, while never getting arrested, without being business savvy.

By T. Styles

Gina's kindness of saving Banks' life came at a cost. And that fee revealed itself when upon waking, it became obvious that Banks didn't remember his past.

Using his memory loss to her advantage, she decided to mold him into the woman she wanted him to be. Besides, she had already kidnapped Banks' twin boys and brought them to the Petit Estate to make things more believable about him being a mother.

About him being female.

Since she was severely sinister, she also lured two of his older children to her mansion, who she kept a secret from Banks by keeping them in the attic. The reason was simple, they alone knew where she'd taken Banks, and Gina didn't want anyone ruining the bond she was building with a granddaughter she had grown to love.

But there was one person on earth who Gina feared would resurface and foil her plan. It was Banks' best friend, Mason Louisville. Whom he had not only grown up with, but who many argued that although Banks was attracted to women, that he cared deeply for his old friend.

On the other hand, it was no question that Mason was very much in love with Banks. Besides, as a preteen, Mason was the one and only man Banks ever had sex with. And Mason held onto this undying love, even after he thought his best friend was dead.

This love was only compounded since there was the issue of Mason being the father to the twin boys, due to swapping his sperm from the original donor's, which was a story too cringey to dig up.

Still, they had history.

But now things were definitely different.

The ball room was slightly dim and decked out with gold and crystal chandeliers. Banquet tables were dripped in embroidered cream-colored linen cloths that hosted silver buckets heavy with ice and champagne. All of the tables were surrounded by millionaires, all coming to see the empress of Strong Curls International.

After a speaker exited the stage, slowly Blaire Petit approached the glass podium again. Her walk was forced in a feminine stride that somehow still appeared sure.

Wearing a red bateau neck long sleeved evening dress, her loose curly hair brushed her shoulders, and her face was stroked lightly, with a breath of makeup. Mainly because she didn't care for the frivolous act of painting one's face. And at the same

18

time, every suitor in the room felt the beauty didn't need any enhancements.

"First I want to say thank you again for joining me tonight for the LOVE WHO YOU ARE dinner gala. My grandmother, who couldn't be here tonight because she's ill, also sends her love." She wore a beauty pageant smile. Stiff but sincere. "All around the world children of color are often persecuted for their yellow and brown skin tones. And we here at Petit Enterprises want to do everything in our power to change this awful stigma. To show them their beautiful colors. And it starts with you good people today."

The room erupted in applause.

She raised her hand and they quieted down slowly. "Tonight, thanks to your extreme generosity, we have already raised over twenty million dollars. This money will be used not only to provide hair and skin care products to young women and men in the neighborhoods that need them the most, but also to provide job and housing opportunities to their families. All while their hair is looking good of course."

More applause. Lots of laughter.

"What about the main prize!" Todd Mulier yelled from across the room while raising his champagne glass. The heir to a billion-dollar real estate firm, he was in his early twenties, blonde and blue eyed.

He also wanted Blaire badly.

She chuckled and pushed down the embarrassment she always felt, when a man complimented her on her beauty. Words of male adoration brought her extreme anxiety, but she didn't know why.

She took a deep breath and raised her hand. "Okay, okay, Todd. We're getting there." More laughter. "Yes, I have agreed to auction myself off on a date..." More excitement. "...to the highest bidder of course."

"I'd like to start off the bid!" Unites King yelled from across the room. He owned the largest law firm in the state of Maryland. Raising his hand, he said, "Fifty thousand dollars!"

More excitement.

"Okay, the bid will start at fifty." She said in a low voice to a crowd that was clearly looking forward to what she deemed an embarrassing moment. "Do we have another—."

"Sixty thousand dollars," Todd said raising his glass from the back.

"Seventy thousand," Unites interjected.

"Eighty..."

By T. Styles

The bidding continued to go up until it reached three hundred thousand dollars. Although at first the room was lighthearted, most believed that Unites should relent and let the young man have his day. Besides, they knew the heiress would never take him seriously anyway. So, what was wrong with him spending a little time in her company?

They also hoped that the young man would refrain from tapping too deeply into his quarterly stipend of a million, which he was coming dangerously close to reaching. In fact, if he continued at the rate he was going, there would be barely any money to take her on a dream date.

"Four hundred thousand!" Unites continued.

"Wow...well...I..." she was so embarrassed her statement halted in her throat and her cheeks reddened. "Thank you. Anybody else?"

For a moment, the room silenced, all wondering what Todd would do next.

"Well, since we don't have any more bids—"

"Four hundred fifty!" Todd yelled.

Unites was about to bid again when his friend placed a heavy hand on his shoulder and whispered into his ear. "Let the boy be."

"Fuck that," Unites said softly so that only he could hear. "That woman is single and wealthy.

And I won't have her wasted on some fucking snot nosed kid." Turning around to face the floor again he yelled, "Five hundred thousand!"

Everyone gasped.

Having jumped higher than he thought the boy was willing to go, he sat back coolly in his seat and grinned. Not giving a fuck that he was coming across as a villain.

Having sensed his win since Todd was silent, Unites cleared his throat and stood up. Adjusting his tie, he said, "Well, I guess me, and Ms. Petit are going on a—."

"One million dollars!" A man yelled in the furthest part of the room.

As if someone was shooting, everyone quickly rotated their heads toward the back, to locate the stranger amongst them. Having heard the culture in his voice, they were certain he was a black man.

It didn't take them long to find the handsome incomer. He was dressed in a black on black Hemsworth suit and his eyes were covered behind smoke gray ombre shades. As he sat in his seat, he stroked his neat five o'clock shadow that melted into his dark chocolate skin and allowed his hand to fall heavily onto his glass of whiskey.

He looked like a movie star.

By T. Styles

For a moment Blaire couldn't see the stranger who placed the bid because the crowd was as thick as cotton fields. But when her eyes finally rested on him, a feeling hit hard in her chest. It was the sensation of air being forced upward, making it difficult to breathe.

Suffocating even.

Who is he? She thought.

"Sir, did you, did you say one million dollars?" She asked cautiously.

He nodded, raised his glass and took a sip. "I did."

Blaire looked at Unites and then Todd. Although she was certain they wouldn't go higher, she had to respect the rules of engagement.

Unites responded by clearing his throat, looking around and sitting down. "No, I'm, I'm good."

The room erupted into applause.

"Well, I...I guess we have a winner." Blaire responded, clapping slowly. "I didn't think I was worth that much."

"You're worth more."

Oohs and aahs.

"Sir, thank you for your very, very generous donation. You will make a lot of young men and women happy."

The stranger rose and she felt as if her heart stopped. As he moved closer to the front, another man with a silver briefcase followed behind him like a cape. The stranger in the black suit's walk was strong and effortless.

He knew who he was.

And he looked the fuck good.

If only she could see his eyes. If only she could see his face fully, then she would understand why she felt a type of way. "Is that the...the donation?"

"Yeah." He smiled.

She cleared her throat and shook his hand. But he hung on a bit longer before letting go. "It's a pleasure meeting you."

"I'm Blaire Petit." She responded.

"I know who you are." He paused. "And I'm Mason."

She stood taller and said his name. It tasted like whiskey in her mouth. "Mason. Ma...son."

Why did the name sound so familiar?

He directed the man to place the briefcase on the table next to the podium. "I hope this helps your foundation and your cause. You make me proud."

"Th...thank you. We take checks you know?" She giggled.

By T. Styles

He placed a hand over his chest but dropped it quickly. "I didn't want you held up with the red tape. The paper is all yours though."

She nodded slowly. Everyone else felt drowned out, giving the illusion that they were alone.

"Well, uh, since you won, where did you want to go for the prize?"

He turned around to face the room who was definitely staring in their direction as if they were watching a classic black and white film. "I'm going to give my date to young Todd." He proclaimed loudly, looking back at him.

Todd smiled widely and everyone clapped.

A new hero was born.

Blaire was disappointed.

But why?

He turned to face her again. "Good evening, Blaire. It was nice meeting the new you." With that he turned and walked out.

Leaving her in awe.

CHAPTER ONE

They had been kept captive in an attic for two years...

And it was starting to take its toll on their spirits in the most inhumane ways.

The blinds were drawn in the garret as Minnesota sat on the floor, reading Spacey a story from a book they found in the walls called, *A Sad Girl's Love*. Their grandmother Angela Petit, who was Blaire's mother, was also held captive in the same attic.

Before she escaped, she hid various books in different locations, including one called *Brainwash Love* by *Gemma Holmes*, which appeared to hold the key to what needed to be done to escape.

This selfless act of hiding books that would later be found by her granddaughter, saved her life.

Since the psychotic book originally belonged to Gina, who didn't know it was missing many years ago, the brother and sister read from its pages daily. In the end they reasoned that being submissive was the best way to escape and so they tried to conform.

By T. Styles

Hard.

But so far it hadn't worked.

Since they never left the room, the smell was dank, the air moist and the space dark, because Spacey had long since avoided opening the window which overlooked the secluded massive land surrounding the Petit Estate.

Declaring that looking outside made him sad, while at the same time reminding him that they would never be free. So, Minnesota respected his wishes, choosing only to gaze at the garden when he was asleep.

Much had changed since they first arrived.

Minnesota had gotten thicker, although unlike in the months prior, her newfound pounds had fallen into the right places. Her breasts, hips and butt area, making it apparent that she was of childbearing age. Her vanilla colored complexion was a bit rosy but not as clear as it had been when she took milk baths.

Spacey, on the other hand, was much smaller, having lost fifteen or so pounds. His face was also hairy, and his frame gaunt, but Minnesota was happy that at least he was alive. His cream-colored skin ashy. Because it was evident that Gina Petit appeared to want to hate him greatly.

"*The little girl had forgotten how much she loved the doll.*" Minnesota read from the book. "*…even its cheap plastic hair, that would thicken and scratch the skin with the slightest amount of hot water. And still, when she lost her doll, she longed to see it's face again. She longed the days where she would search her room for its missing leg for hours. And she missed the satisfaction she would receive when she found it and popped it back in place. She missed her old friend and it was only when she lost her new one that she realized this fact.*" She slammed the book and took a deep breath. "We'll stop there for today." She sighed. "So, what do you think?"

Spacey got up and sat on his bed. "I can't believe I let you read me that dumb story once a week."

"You are so grumpy."

She giggled and dropped the book on the floor, before jumping in bed with him. Crawling up behind him, she tickled him profusely until he forced out a laugh.

Turning around he faced her. "Stop being silly, pretty girl."

For a moment, they embraced silence. Staring into one another's eyes. "I'm glad you're here with me, Spacey."

"Why you say that?" He frowned and scratched his face, leaving red claw marks on his light skin. "Because you know they want me gone and I should be dead by now?"

"I'm serious. I mean, it's been two years and without you, Spacey, I wouldn't be able to survive. And—."

"Stop." He rolled his eyes. "See, that's why I didn't want you reading them dumb ass books to me. You always get in your feelings and shit."

"How are you?"

He rolled his eyes again. "I'm fineeeeeeee, Minnesota."

"I didn't say you weren't. I—."

"You're checking my temperature." He paused. "Wondering if I'm still handling it all."

"That's because I hate how they do you when they take you away. The beatings. The holding back on your food. Why so mean to my brother?"

"Well I'm done fighting with them." He looked defeated and it broke her heart. "For real this time."

She frowned. "What does that mean? And what goes on when they take you away?"

"Leave it alone." He sat up in bed and leaned his back against the wall.

She sat next to him. "So, does this mean you'll like, not fight anymore? Is that what you're—."

There was a knock at the door. Although Spacey was first in the past to greet the maid and Butler, mostly ready for war, lately he was resigned. As if getting weaker. As if deciding to give up on life.

Minnesota quickly walked to the door and stood five feet back per their instructions. "It's clear." She announced.

Just then keys could be heard jingling and the door opened. On the other side Frances, the maid, appeared. Her graying hair was pushed up in a weak ass bun, which was lopsided and unsure of itself. And her pale face was covered in a surgical mask; she was pushing a food cart with Carl, the butler, standing in the rear. He was a tall white man with oily black hair who was very much giving off the Addams Family vibes.

Pushing the tray inside, Frances lifted the silver cloches. The moment she did, the smells wafted into Minnesota and Spacey's nose, awakening in them an urge to eat. One plate had a fresh steak roll with fries. The other held a half-eaten steak roll, which was tainted with orange lipstick.

It was Gina's color.

It was Gina's trash.

Frances left and Minnesota turned around, facing her brother who stood directly behind her. So close her face bumped into his chest as she inhaled his musty odor.

"It's time to eat." She said in a low voice.

"It looks good." He said dryly before grabbing the scraps plate and flopping on his bed.

Minnesota sighed, grabbed her plate, labeled with her name of course, and sat next to him.

"Why you over here? Go sit on your bed." He grabbed the half-eaten sandwich, but her hand weighed down on it heavily.

Quickly she took her full sandwich and pulled it in half. Dividing her meal, she gave him one piece and kept the other. Next she tossed the used sandwich in the trash before sitting next to him again.

She loved to stay near.

"You don't have to eat her scraps. Fuck her."

Splitting a meal made for one, was the reason he lost so much weight. But she refused to have her brother eat garbage, when she would gladly share.

Grabbing her sandwich, she took a bite but paused when she saw he wasn't eating. "What's wrong? I thought you were hungry. You know they'll be back for the trays. So, hurry."

"You didn't have to do that."

"Yes, I did. I don't...I don't like what they're trying to do to you. What they're trying to do to us. You're my brother, Spacey."

"Technically we don't share blood so—."

"I don't care, Spacey." She plopped her sandwich on the plate as she spoke with her whole heart. "Don't talk to me like that again."

"I'm not trying to. I just don't want you getting hurt because of me."

"I won't get hurt, Spacey."

"You can't say that. Just because you've been okay now, it doesn't mean you will be always, Minnesota." He put his plate on the side of the bed. "I mean think about it, the food trays have been coming later in the day. Only once. And we still don't know if they're spraying something in the air since they wear face masks every now and again. What if the house is poisoned? And this is some wild ass experiment."

32 By T. Styles

She placed her hand on his leg. "I'll be fine. We'll be fine. And maybe...maybe when Dad gets better, he'll—."

"I don't think you can depend on Pops, Minnesota."

She frowned. "What...why not? We always could depend on him in the past."

"Because I think he's gone. Why else would he not come for us?"

"Well I'm holding onto hope." She raised her head high. "If you don't mind." She nudged him playfully with her shoulder.

"I think hope is a dangerous thing." He hung his head low. "Very dangerous."

She placed her finger under his chin and pushed upward. "Head to the sky, King. We're Wales'. And they can never take away who we really are inside. No matter how hard they try."

He smiled, winked and kissed her on the forehead. "I hear you. Let's eat."

The door opened and the maid entered. "Spacey, Gina will see you now."

Minnesota forced back a gasp, knowing that this was just another instance where he would be beaten for no reason. It didn't help things that

Spacey never told her all he went through during those private visits away from the attic.

"Spacey..." Minnesota whispered.

He grabbed her hand. "I'll be fine. I always am."

Gina sat in her bed, propped up by so many pillows behind her upper body, that she appeared to be bending forward. Her lips smeared with too much orange lipstick. Her favorite. When her vintage style phone with the gold handle rang, she answered.

"Hello..."

"Gina, it's me."

She threw her head back in annoyance, but it bounced forward like a ball into a wall. "What do you want, Marshall?"

"I, I need your help."

She grinned evilly. "Do you need my help or my money?"

Silence.

By T. Styles

She shook her head. "When you left me those years back, I warned you that you could never return if you did. Didn't I?"

"I left because I wanted to see my family again. I left because it had been years since I'd been in contact with them and I missed them greatly."

"I loved you. And you betrayed me."

"No, you also raised me." He said a bit louder. "And then you used me."

"You were living in a foster home, fucking other young men, and I saved you."

"No, Gina. You molded me when I was a kid, just to be *your* sex toy. Forced me to live in the attic until I did what you called, '*right by you*'."

"And you enjoyed it too."

"No, I didn't. It was either fuck you or die upstairs. And I chose to die in your bed instead." He paused. "I did my job. For years without question. And the one time I wanted to see my family you punished me. And now...now I'm broke and living on the streets and you won't help me."

"What do you want, Marshall?" She simply didn't have time for him. "Hurry now. I'm bored."

"Can I come home?"

"Your home is no longer here." She laughed. "It's in Mexico remember? You made your decision."

He sighed long and hard. "If you don't put money into my banking account by the end of the day, I'll tell the news about the people in the attic. I'll tell Banks who he really is too."

Gina tried to sit up, but again, the pillows bounced her forward. "Are you threatening me?"

"No, I'm promising to react. That's all." He gave her his banking account information, which she recorded with pen and paper. "You have the money, Gina. Isn't a million worth my silence? And worth keeping your secret safe?"

When she ended the call, Frances and Carl brought Spacey into the room. "I'll be right outside your doorway if you need me." Carl said.

She nodded and he closed the door.

Spacey stood with his hands behind his back.

"You look bad." She said.

"What do you want, Gina?"

"I want you to massage my feet. They have been aching badly and I miss your touch."

"Is my father alive?"

"What did I tell you about asking me questions? Haven't you learned that the more questions you

36   By T. Styles

ask, the more I will hurt you?" She paused. "Now, will you massage my feet, or will you be taking lashes this evening?"

Spacey walked over to the bed and yanked the covers down, exposing her withered body in the gray nightgown. She wiggled her toes for fun which annoyed him like shit. "The oil is on my dresser. You know the routine."

Slowly he moped toward the dresser.

While he was away, she raised her gown, exposing her gray vagina. Her pussy lips had thinned over the years, causing them to weigh on the bed like heavy change purses. This gave off the awkward illusion of her clit pushing outward, almost like a mini dick.

When Spacey returned and saw her snatch, he rolled his eyes and snatched her foot. Each toe had its own personal patch of hair which caused him to want to yell inside.

"Easy, big boy." She grinned. "I don't mind a little pain but not on my feet."

Rubbing oil on his hands like Mr. Miyagi, he massaged her right foot first. Her skin was so wrinkled, it felt like it would slide off.

"You hate me, but there is a way for things to change."

Silence.

"All you have to do, is be there for me, in ways I can't be for myself. You do that, and I will restore your body to its normal state. Strong. Muscular. I promise."

Silence.

"You may ask me a question now."

"What do you want?"

"It's a funny thing, my legs don't work but my pussy still does. And one of the things that always got me right, was a good licking."

He tried to hold down his vomit.

Gina wasn't a bad looking woman, even in her old age. What disgusted him about her beyond all, was the evil in her eyes.

The malice in her heart.

"I don't want to."

"We had an arrangement. You would continue to lick me right, and I will continue to give you my scraps, and feed your sister healthy portions. Are you going against your promise? Or do you want her to slowly die too?"

"I don't want to do what you want anymore. And last time you...last time you peed in my mouth." He wanted to throw up just remembering the thought.

38   By T. Styles

She giggled. "Aw, come on. I won't do it a—."

"I said no!"

She glared at him for five minutes as he continued to stroke her feet. No talking. Barely even breathing. Just a death stare.

"Since you can't remember how to treat me, I may forget more and more to feed you and Minnesota." She raised her head high. "Carl!"

The door came flying open. "Yes, ma'am?"

"Get this nigger out of my presence."

Carl stomped toward Spacey. "Yes, ma'am right away!" He yanked him off the bed.

"Oh, and call Officer Logan. I have a job I need him to handle."

CHAPTER TWO

Blaire was in her twin sons', Ace and Walid's bedroom...

And let's just say, their territory was nothing short of magical. Larger than the master suite, it resembled a little fortress for the young kings. One side of the room had matching racecar beds while the other side was separated by a wall, where a mini movie screen, complete with theater style chairs was present.

Having every luxury clothing piece known to man, the twins were groomed well, and the moment you saw them, you could tell that they came from extreme wealth. It was in the way their healthy shiny curls bounced as they played. The way the sun kissed their milky clear skin tone, courtesy of weekly facials. And it was in the way the gold chains dangled around their necks and sparkled.

But for Walid things hit a bit deeper.

His eyes spoke of things his mind couldn't fathom. Of the power steeped in his Louisville and Wales bloodline. And he moved about the world, often as if he'd been here before. Almost as if he'd

By T. Styles

seen the atrocities due to the blood shed that his parents participated in, in an effort to push coke and gain wealth on the streets of Baltimore.

Ace, on the other hand, was more relaxed and fun, which was always a delight to those he came around. His love was free and available to all, while Walid appeared to treat all those he didn't know from a distance, holding his heart at ransom.

Trusting only a few.

No, scratch that.

Trusting no one.

The twins and Blaire were sitting on the edge of the bed when Gina rolled inside with her wheelchair. It sounded clunky and old, but she didn't want a new one. On the back of it was an oxygen tank that kept her alive. Her bones had weakened since contracting the virus in the air, but her mental strength was as strong as ever.

Blaire placed the book down on the bed. She had an early Alicia Keys soft, boyish vibe, that made her all the more appealing.

Ace quickly hopped out of bed, rushed over and hugged Gina tightly. "Hello, great-grandmother!"

"Aw, sweetheart, your hugs are the highlight to my day."

"I love you." He sang, giving of his whole heart.

As she rustled his thick curly hair that smelled of the vanilla scented product they produced, she eyed Walid who was glaring their way. "And I love you more, Ace."

When Ace ran back to his bed, she smiled at Walid who remained seated. The child simply couldn't be bothered to talk to the old woman.

"Hello, son." Gina said to him.

Silence.

"So, you still aren't going to speak to me?" Gina asked.

"Walid, go hug your great-grandmother." Blaire was embarrassed as fuck. He was a pro at hoarding the woman.

"Nah."

Blaire looked down at him and frowned. "*Nah*?" Blaire giggled. "Where you hear that from? We speak in full words in this house. You know that."

He looked up at her. "I heard it from a few places."

"Well what have you been watching because that's not—"

"He's been spending too much time with Carl." Gina shook her head. "Apparently he thinks his butler duties involve being with my great grandson during his free time. I'm going to have to educate him properly on what's required."

Blaire looked over at her. "So, Carl lets him talk like this?"

"I wouldn't say lets him, but he spends a lot of time with him after school." She sighed. "Frances told me." She laughed.

Blaire frowned. "What about her? Apparently, she thinks her maid duties include watching their every move." Blaire didn't care for the maid at all.

Gina waved the air when she saw the troubled look on Blaire's face. "Don't worry. I'll handle things."

Blaire sighed and looked at her son. "Walid, go hug your great-grandmother."

He looked up at her with his light eyes. He couldn't believe she was back on the hugging shit. "But I don't want to." He looked back at Gina. "I don't like how she feels."

Blaire frowned. "Now what is that supposed to mean?"

He shrugged. "I used full words this time. You still don't understand me?"

Blaire was done with him. The boy was too brilliant for his own good.

"Well, I don't care what you used." She glared. "Get over there and hug her." She paused. "Now."

The way her words fell from her tongue were forceful and filled with bass. Almost as if she had reconnected with who she was before life changed. Almost as if she were, well, Banks Wales.

Irritated like a hungry man standing in line at a buffet, he stomped toward the old woman and slammed his arms around her roughly like a handcuff on a wrist. When he was done, he removed them quickly. The embrace hurt, because Walid above all things was cock strong.

The baby did little push-ups for fun.

"Ouch..." Gina said honestly.

"Walid, be careful. You can hurt her."

He hopped on his bed and yanked the covers up to his chin. "I told you I didn't wanna do it."

"Again, with the broken words?" Blaire said.

"Oh, I'm sorry, I told you I didn't want to do it." Walid pulled the sheets over his face, vowing to look at no one for the rest of the night.

Blaire had enough and put them to sleep and cut off the lights. Pushing Gina's chair out the door she walked her to her own room. "I'm sorry, grandmother. I wish I knew why he acts that way."

By T. Styles

"Something in his genes." Gina said, taking a direct shot at Mason Louisville.

Blaire nodded and opened Gina's bedroom door, before helping her inside. "That's one of the things that bothers me. I mean, I know the cancer caused me to have memory loss but times like this I wish I could recall anything about the past, so I could help more. It's the scariest thing in the world to not know who you are."

Gina grabbed her hand and pulled her in front of her. Out of respect, Blaire always lowered her height when standing. Besides, she was tall.

"Listen, the past doesn't matter when your future is bright." She placed a cold hand on her face. "You have everything you want in life."

She looked down. "Not everything." She sighed.

"What do you mean?"

"I feel...I feel like something's missing. I feel like I'm not myself and its tearing me apart." She looked down. "Almost as if just by living, I'm lying to myself. Like I'm a fraud. And I—."

"You aren't a fraud. You are your most authentic self." Gina interjected. "Trust me. I knew you since you were a baby." She lied. "And you were always a sad little girl and woman. That changed. Now you are truly living in your best state." She sighed. "Now, honey, be a dear and bring me my pain medicine." She pointed at her bed table before rubbing her head. Whenever Blaire got to talking about the past, the old bird got silly with aches and pains. "The tall bottle."

Blaire got up and walked across the large room. Instead of using the feminine gait she practiced with Gina for well over a year, she bopped like a dude about to move that work. It was very masculine. And because she was wearing a dress, it seemed odd and out of place.

"Blaire, your walk again." She pointed at her with a crooked finger. "Glide, dear. Don't tromp."

Blaire stopped and sighed. "I'm sorry...I don't...I don't understand why I move like that sometimes. It's like...second nature." She grabbed the pills and poured her a glass of ice water that the maid brought in earlier.

"I told you why. You had always been a tomboy. Even your husband found your mannerisms peculiar, but he loved you all the same."

Gina had constructed a cloud of lies, necessary to create the world she needed Blaire to occupy.

Walking more with the hips, and dips, she said, "I wish I could remember him." She sighed long and hard. "I feel like if he were here, and the car

By T. Styles

accident didn't take his life, then maybe he could help me understand why I'm so sad. And why Walid is so angry."

Gina handed her the pill bottle which she put on the floor.

Grabbing her hand, she said, "First off Walid was too young to remember his father. If he saw the man today, he would walk right past him."

"Saw him today?"

"And don't beat up yourself." Gina ran over her slip up. "You have come so far, and I want the best for you. Things will work out. You will find another man who will give up the world for you."

Personally, it sounded gross and again Blaire didn't know why. She just simply wasn't in the man search business. "Maybe."

"So, how was the benefit? I'm told you raised more than enough funds."

Blaire thought about the stranger at the gala but for some reason, she decided not to tell her his name.

For now, he would remain her little secret.

"It was fine."

THE NEXT DAY

The maid and butler were pushing a food cart toward the elevator. Right before they entered, Gina rolled up to them. She lifted both silver cloche's off the plates and glared up at them.

There was too much food as far as she was concerned.

She removed a chicken thigh that was half eaten, leaving only some of its flesh behind. "This is too much meat. Remember, rations are very important. I want less for both of them these days."

As she continued to school her employees, Walid bopped up and tried to get onto the elevator.

"No, Walid," she grabbed him by the arm, her long thick nails digging into his flesh. "You aren't allowed upstairs. Ever."

He snatched away and got busy. "Don't touch me. I go where I please." With that he ran away leaving all three on pause.

CHAPTER THREE

M ason was in the foyer, about to get into his car when he realized he forgot his phone. When he walked into his room, he was shocked to see his girlfriend Dasher, going through his cell with quick swipes upward.

"What the fuck is you doing?" He slammed the door.

She jumped and hid his phone behind her back. "N...nothing."

He walked closer, a glare on his handsome chocolate face. "What you got behind your back then? It bet not be my shit."

She looked down and slowly extended the phone.

It was his shit.

"I'm sorry...I was just...I mean—."

"Snooping on me." He snatched it away. "What the fuck is wrong with you? Huh? I told you how I feel about shit like this and you disrespect anyway?"

"I'm so sorry." She covered her mouth with her fingertips and peddled her bottom lip like she was playing piano.

"That ain't good enough." He looked down at his screen and dropped it in his pocket. His nerves were rattled because he didn't think she had the sneak DNA in her spirit.

"I get that." She threw her arms up in the air. "But lately you've been disconnected. Taking long drives away from me. Leaving me in the house to deal with...with...everything alone."

"Deal with what, Dasher?"

"I just said being alone! You not even listening to me right now!" She walked up to him and grabbed his hand. "Mason, I would've never moved here had I known you didn't want me in your life."

He dragged a lazy hand down his face and plopped in the chair in his room. It's true, he had been disconnected lately. But his mind was on the twins and Banks. And the way he saw it, nothing else mattered.

When he first discovered his sons were posted up in a mansion, he was shocked when he saw Banks too. For over a year he was told Banks was dead. And so, his purpose was to locate his sons and bring them home now that his life was stable.

But when he found out that his friend and the only person he ever really loved was alive and well, he was stunned. So stunned, that he didn't bother coming home for a week, which sent Dasher and his ex-wife, who were both staying at the Louisville estate, on a frenzy of emotions.

But he didn't care.

In the beginning he wanted to snatch Banks away from Gina's grasp, and force him to remember who he really was. Instead he watched him within the realms of his new life.

From a far, he saw how he interacted with their sons and the business, and it became obvious that not only was his friend no longer Banks Wales, but it was also clear that he had no idea who he was in his former life, otherwise, he would've never been caught in a dress.

And so, he decided to take the slower approach.

He decided to become the person necessary to connect with Blaire in her new world. And when the time was right, he planned to tell her everything. About the time they spent as kids growing up in Baltimore. About his wife. About the children that he didn't know about....Harris, Joey. Along with Spacey and Minnesota, who he was certain were murdered.

He would even bring up his new baby girl Blakeslee.

But he had to be slow, realizing that shocking her into the past would do more harm in the future.

"I never said I didn't want you, Dasher."

She sat on the bed across from him. "Well that's how I feel. I mean, is it another woman? Because I can be whoever you want me to be. You know that! There's no reason to go outside of our relationship."

"What I tell you about talking like that?" He glared.

"About talking like what? You mean me trying to fight for you? Because by now you know me well enough to know I will be a chameleon if you need."

She was yuck.

"You know what, there is something I been wanting to rap to you about."

"Okay, I'm listening."

"I don't think you should be living here."

Her eyes widened. "Is it because of Derrick and Shay? Because I know they had a problem with me living here before, but we're cool now and—."

"It's not about them."

She shook her head. "Okay, then what is it?"

"I can't be responsible for your feelings. I know you need someone you can confide in. Someone

By T. Styles

who can make you believe that everything will be okay. But the way I'm moving right now, I can't spare any extra emotions."

"Mason, please, please don't do this."

He stood up. "I'm done. I'll set you up with a nice place, so you won't have to worry about shit. But you can't be in my bed."

"I don't want a nice place if you aren't there!"

"That has nothing to do with me, kid." He shrugged. "For real. I'm looking out by setting you free."

"Please, Mason." She dropped to her knees. "I'll die if you—."

"This what the fuck I'm talking about." He pointed at her as if someone shat on the floor. "I'm sick of this weak shit. If a nigga say he don't want you, you should say fuck it and move on. And then you wonder why I treat you the way I do sometimes."

"Mason, I—."

"I'm on my way out. I got something to—."

"I'm pregnant!"

He paused and turned around to face her. "What?"

"Just what I said. I'm pregnant." She used the bed to help her stand up, since Mason wasn't interested in the small chore. "That's why I been wanting to talk to you. That's why I wanted to move here because...because I didn't want to go through this alone." She rubbed her flat belly.

He scratched his head. "Wow."

"Wow?" She shrugged. "I just told you I'm pregnant and that's all you can say?"

"I mean...you fucking me up right now with all of this emotional shit." He sighed.

"Emotional shit?"

"If I'm being honest, and I'm not calling you a liar, but if I'm being honest, it sounds a little on the half that the moment I put you out, all of a sudden you pregnant with child and shit." He shook his head.

She frowned and wiped her wet nose with the back of her hand. "I thought you were a man."

"Don't question my masculinity."

"I ain't talking about your masculinity, nigga!" She clapped four times for effect. "I'm talking about you being cold and heartless. I knew you had an edge. And to be honest it's something I liked about you. Even though I knew it could hurt me but this...this is way too much. You are, well, evil."

"You right."

"What does that fucking mean?"

By T. Styles

"It means I'm going about this the wrong way."
He threw his hand up, feeling like he had a few
moments to spare. Looking at his watch he said,
"So, how long you know and shit like that?"

"I've missed three periods so—."

"Why didn't you hit me up when you first
missed a cycle?"

"It's my body."

"But you want it to be my problem?" He
laughed once.

"A problem?" She tilted her head. "So, you
think our baby is a problem?"

"Nah, what I think is I can't deal with this right
now. I tried for a few seconds and whatever, but
now my ass itches. But I'll let you know when I can
rap later though." He stomped out.

CHAPTER FOUR

Mason's son, Derrick, was playing with his six-month-old son he named Patrick after his brother Patterson who was murdered by his other brother Howard. It was a messy situation. But then again, the Louisville's were a messy group of niggas.

The baby was an easy-going kid which he appreciated considering the fact that these days he felt like a single father.

Shay Wales, after giving birth, made it known that she had no intentions on being a full-time mom. Especially since their relationship was on the rocks. And since he was raised around his mother, who lived for her kids, he was stunned.

Didn't every woman want to have a baby?

No. Not really.

When Patrick's eyes fluttered indicating he was about to go to sleep, he got up from the bed and grabbed his cell phone on the dresser. When he was escorted to Shay's voicemail, he took a deep breath.

"Listen, you been out all night. Fuck is going on? You in a relationship, aren't you?"

When he thought about how he sounded, he deleted the message and tried again. Clearing his throat, he said, "Listen, you gonna make me fuck you up if you don't pick up this phone. You think I'm a scab? Is that what you think? You think you can walk the fuck..."

He deleted the voice message reasoning that, that one sounded worse.

Taking a deep breath, he again tried his hand. "When I see you, I'ma smack the shit out of you."

With that, he sent the message.

While his son was sleeping, he walked quietly out of his room and toward his mother's room. Even though she was no longer with his father, Jersey stayed in the house preferring to be around family.

It wasn't like they were helping her with her daughter. They were more trouble than they were worth if we're being honest. But still she stayed.

At first everybody thought it would be beef in the mansion, seeing as though Dasher was living there too. But Jersey didn't care. She had her own troubles that required her attention.

Knocking on his mother's door, he waited impatiently for her to answer. Feet tapping. Pacing. He was a mess.

When the door opened and he saw his little sister Blakeslee playing in the playpen, he walked over to her and lifted her up. More to have something to do than anything else. The toddler's eyes always lit up when she saw her brother, despite there being no direct bloodline.

"What you want, Derrick?" Jersey asked, hands on the hip. Her hair sat in a messy bun on top of her head, but she was still beautiful. This was amazing considering her light brown skin was stained with baby food and she looked exhausted.

"Hold up, why you coming at me like that?"

"Because I know you. You only come to my room when you want something. So, what is it?"

"Please don't act like I don't got love for my sister, ma. Like I don't come check on her from time to time."

"I didn't say all that. What I did say was what I said. Now what you want?"

"I can't find Shay. She out here in these streets with her pussy out and I feel like yoking her ass."

Jersey sighed and flopped on the edge of the bed. "Why are you still with that girl? Huh? It's obvious she doesn't want to be with you. Just let her go."

"You know why she's acting out." He pointed.

By T. Styles

"I do." She nodded. "Nobody feels the pain more than me of Banks being gone. Of my sons being dead. And even of Minnesota and Spacey's disappearance. Let's not even talk about Howard being missing. But disrespect is another question all together and she has zero respect in that area, Derrick. She's a garbage can."

"She's still my girl."

"I get that, son. But I hate seeing you like this."

He nodded and put the baby back in the playpen. He hoped she wouldn't cry when he let her go.

She was good.

Didn't feel like being held anyway.

"Listen, ma, I'm going to make some decisions about my relationship soon."

"What does that mean?"

He shrugged and looked at the floor as if seeking an answer. "I'm gonna call her on her shit. And if she don't know how to act, then I guess, I mean, I guess it's over between us."

She sighed. "You won't be able to do that."

"You don't know me as good as you think you do."

"I know you better than you know yourself. I gave birth to you remember?"

He sighed. "Listen, just watch him for five minutes, ma. I put him to sleep and everything. I won't be out long, I promise."

"Derrick, you don't know how hard it is to watch two babies under the age of three at the same time. I—."

"For me, ma. Please."

There was no use. He would be on bended knee in a minute if she didn't relent. "Go ahead, boy. But don't be out all night. And don't be fighting that girl in the streets either. It's tough out here for your brand."

"Nah, I'm just gonna find her and bring her ass home. Period." He slithered out the door.

Tucked inside a fifty-story building, with mirror windows throughout, stood the empress Blaire Petit, of Strong Curls Inc a subsidiary of Petit Enterprises. To say she turned a failing business in as little as two years into a mega house would be an understatement. She not only increased

By T. Styles

profit margins by over one hundred percent, she also excelled as a leader in every area of the brand. When new product was created, she hustled hard to get it to the streets.

It was as if she were a natural born entrepreneur.

The employees of Strong Curls hung around the table, waiting for Blaire to walk inside to conduct her daily board meeting. Since the boardroom was surrounded with glass walls, they could see her talking to an employee outside of her massive office.

Looking at her body mechanics from afar, John Taylor, head of marketing, leaned over to Marvin Heights, who was the head of design. "She's beautiful but something about her is off." John whispered.

"Why do you say that?"

"I mean look at her." They both gazed her way. She was wearing a black designer pantsuit with pearls that hung a bit low like a dope boy chain. "Whenever she talks to a woman, she always touches the small of their backs. As if protecting them from something."

"Well, she is tall." Marvin laughed.

"Nah, it's something else."

"What else could it be?" Joanna interjected, whipping her luscious blond hair out of her face. They hadn't known that Blaire's best friend was ear hustling, otherwise they would have been more cautious.

John cleared his throat. "Nothing..."

"Oh, I already know you're talking about nothing. Because the last thing you want is to lose your fucking job for speaking ill about our boss."

They held their heads down just as Blaire walked inside, smiling per usual. She loved everything about making money. "Okay, how is everyone today?"

Blaire looked at John and Marvin who cleared their throats.

"Good, boss..." they said one by one.

Blaire pressed her hands together. "Perfect, because by now you are aware that the product launch for Banana Curls drops next week. And I want to make sure we campaign right."

John raised his hand. "Yeah, that's what I wanted to talk to you about too."

Blaire took a seat to respect her employee. "Okay, I'm listening."

"It's just that you've rejected all of the models I presented for the promo ads for both our television

By T. Styles

and print campaigns. Which is bizarre because not many CEO's want to bother themselves with such minor issues."

"I'm involved because I care. And I didn't approve your selections because I want a variety of beautiful women. In all shades and shapes. Like we talked about last week." She sat back in her chair. "I thought I made myself clear."

"But we assumed, historically speaking rather, that even the black community equates beauty with lighter skin. So, we wanted to—."

"John..." She was heated but chose to remain calm. "I'm aware of what you believe. I've spoken to my grandmother about these concerns in great detail. Especially when you tried to go over my head. But your assumptions are false at best. Which is one of the reasons I rejected the models. Bring me a variety. Or bring me nothing. And then I'll find someone who can."

Silence.

"I get that but what's wrong with making the variety of models with lighter skin tones so that—."

Blaire raised her hand. "Nah, let me be direct, my nigga."

Everyone in the room gasped.

But Blaire was shocked for a different reason.

Earlier in the week she got at Walid for using the word '*nah*', only to come quick with the same term once being disrespected. Did she do this before without knowing which caused Walid to overhear her?

Clearing her throat she said, "That is my product. And these are my people. And while I appreciate the level at which you believe you know what my people want, you are off. We are in the hair care business, John. And I want my people to see themselves in full color on these billboards." She smiled wider. "Now find me some new models who depict every shape and tone by the end of the day, or you're fired." She focused on Joanna. "Ready for lunch?"

Joanna winked. "Born ready, boss."

The apartment was magnificent. With floor to ceiling windows in the living room and bedrooms, the property was created to take your breath away.

By T. Styles

And it all belonged to Banks' son, who had gotten caught up on drugs, Joey Wales.

The crib was courtesy of Mason.

After making sure everything was as ordered, Mason followed the agent throughout the apartment until they got to the living room. "I really do believe this place will serve your needs, sir. It truly is magnificent."

"It ain't for me." Mason walked up to the floor to ceiling window that overlooked the city.

"Oh, I just—."

"It's for my nephew." He sighed. "And when he gets back in town, I need to have everything perfect. I'm having his furniture brought up on Friday if everything goes well with the paperwork. You should—." Mason's cell phone rang. "I gotta take this."

"Oh, of course." The agent left the apartment and Mason answered.

"How are you, Joey?" He leaned against the wall.

"I'm good, well, as good as I can be in rehab."

He nodded. "So are you..."

"Clean?"

Mason smiled. "Yeah."

"I am." He sighed. "And to be honest, I haven't felt this good at any point in my life. *Ever.* Even when Pops put me through his rehab process it did more harm to my nerves than good. Increased my anxiety and—."

The thing was, no Banks slander would be tolerated.

"He was trying to help you, Joey. Have a little respect."

"I know. I...I didn't mean it like that."

He nodded. "Good, because sometimes people don't realize what love looks like, just because it's dressed a little differently."

"You're right. I don't mean any disrespect."

Mason walked toward the other wall and leaned against it. "So, when are you coming home? I have a new place for you. It's an apartment in the city and it's nice, Joey. Got a good rate because of everything going on. Paid up for two years."

"Oh, uh, I'm staying here, Unc."

He frowned. "Wait, you're staying in Arizona?" He stood up straight.

"Yes."

"But your people ain't out there, Joey." He glared. "Everything and everybody who loves you is out here." He tossed up his free arm.

By T. Styles

"What's there for me? *Really*? I mean, Pops is dead. Minnesota and Spacey are gone too. And my mother...my mother was murdered." He pulled back a little, feeling himself a bit choked up. "So, tell me, what I got to come back for, Unc?"

Mason felt gut punched.

He was waiting for him.

They may not have been blood, but he wanted to keep the bond the Lou's and Wales' had together. At the end of the day their relationship wasn't perfect, but he cared deeply for the young bull. "You're right."

"Don't worry, Unc, I'll come visit. I just...I just..."

"I get it, son. I get it. You don't have to make excuses for becoming a man." He shook his head. "I wish I could've muscled up and been who I needed to be when I was in my early twenties. I'm proud of you."

"For real?"

"Yes." He nodded. "You took a different route in life, but you still found your way. And I want you to...I guess I wanna say..."

"I love you too." Joey responded.

Mason smiled and forced back his emotions just as the agent reentered the apartment. He didn't even give a nigga a chance to piss if he so desired.

Rolling his eyes, he said, "I have to go, Joey. But listen, don't give up on your father yet."

"What do you mean?" There was excitement laced with hope throughout Joey's tone.

Was he alive?

"I mean, never give up on him." Mason cleared his comment up. It was obvious he wanted to keep Banks' being alive a secret. "Remember who you are."

"Oh, okay. I'll talk to you later, Unc."

When he ended the call, the agent approached. "So, do we have a deal?"

Mason thought about his current home situation. How someone always seemed to be around, in the business, in his face, using his toilet. Breathing on his neck. Since Joey wasn't coming back, what would stop him from keeping the place for himself?

"Yes, we have a deal."

The agent tried to shake his hand, but Mason was done with those acts of kindness considering the virus and all. Handshakes were reserved for the most trusted comrades only.

"Oh, I'm sorry. I almost forgot." The agent said tucking his fingertips back into his pocket.

"Not me." He walked toward the door. "Now where do I sign?"

When Mason walked outside of the apartment building, Dasher was leaning against his car stomping her foot. "Can we talk?"

He dragged a hand down his face. "*Can we talk?* How the fuck did you know where I was?"

"I know things, Mason." She rubbed her belly, which appeared even flatter than it was a few days ago.

Was that a six pack?

"And if you don't make time to listen to me, or at least understand me, there will be major issues for you." She continued. "I can make issues for you right now if I want."

"First off stop saying issues." He moved to stuff her back into the car like loose garbage in a packed can, but she couldn't be moved. "Listen, you can't be following me and shit. I don't—."

"HELP! HELLLLLP! HELLP!" She started screaming.

With wide eyes he grabbed her arm while looking around to see if anyone was coming. "What the fuck are you doing? Huh?"

"I'm calling for help!" She said. "Since it's obvious you won't help me by being my man."

He was livid. *Who the fuck was this chick?* Is what he kept asking himself. "You would really pull some shit like that, when you know the climate we in right now for niggas? When you know how hard it is for a black man to—."

"Blah, blah, blah, blah-ba-dee fuck that shit! I'm not going to let you get away from me. I'm not going to let you and whoever the fuck you dating right now, run off into the moon." She reached into her pocket and pulled out the wrinkled pregnancy test results from a doctor's office. "And since I know you have been known to get rid of those you're done with, with the exception of your children and baby mamas, I thought I should add myself to the list."

He looked down at the sheet. It was true. She was pregnant.

By T. Styles

"You either make a place for me in your life, or I will make one for myself." She smiled. "And trust me, it will be a mothafucking *issue* for you."

CHAPTER FIVE

The world was still bizarre due to 'the change' but there was a sense of normalcy returning to some aspects of life. Although masks still donned the faces of many who moved about, most restaurants had resorted to serving meals outside, which made for an awkward experience as Blaire and Joanna walked down the block to pick up their lunches.

"John only acts like that because he has zero friends who hold him accountable." Joanna said. "He's annoying but he does love the business and Petit Enterprises. He spends hours in his office researching different textures of African American hair. So, he—"

"I hear you, but I need John to be a little smarter." Blaire said cutting her off. "To be a little more self-aware. And to know his place." They approached the restaurant's outdoor table. "We're here to pick up the Petit order."

The employee looked at the sheet and nodded. "Yes, your name is right here. One moment please."

When she left Joanna sighed. "I don't understand why you don't send people to get your food. You're damn near a billionaire."

"I don't know either to be honest," she shrugged. "I guess I like being out in the streets."

"I get that but why?"

"I feel better when I'm out, moving about."

Joanna sighed. "I'll be glad when things change in the world. And the virus is gone so—."

"Don't say it."

"How do you know what I'm about to say?" She grinned.

"Because you've said it before a million times. And I don't want you to worry about the future because it doesn't help the present." Her head hung and Blaire touched her chin, raising it slightly. "You'll be fine."

Five minutes later they were sitting inside of Blaire's Range Rover eating Rueben sandwiches with fries. They were delicious too.

"...so, I told him, no, you can't come over." Joanna continued with a mouth full of food. "Even though I wanted to see him."

"What did he do?" Blaire stuffed the other half of the sandwich in the bag. She was already full.

"Because I know he's been trying for a while to get back into your life."

She shrugged. "He popped up over my house anyway. But I was firm, and he left. After I sucked his dick of course."

She laughed. "Well I doubt he got the message if you did all that." Blaire sipped her drink.

"You mean because I played myself like a whore?" She shrugged. "Because I don't exactly have men knocking down the door to get at me if you know what I mean."

"Why do you keep saying that?"

"Because I'm not classically beautiful, Blaire."

Blaire frowned. "Wait, you're serious?"

"Yes."

"Joanna, you're very attractive." She said softly. "Why can't you see that?"

The way she said those words had Joanna feeling a type of way. "I don't know...I mean...I can't see it when I look into a mirror."

"Well I'm telling you that you are a very beautiful woman."

She nodded and took a deep breath. Her whole body seemed to heat up. Blaire knew how to talk to the ladies that was for sure. "Okay, enough of my boring stories. What's going on with you? You seem sad lately."

"Sad?" She frowned. "Really?"

"Yes. I can tell you're here physically, but you seem to be someplace else mentally. So, where are you?"

Blaire nodded. "Have you ever felt that you were another person?"

Joanna thought briefly. "I can't say that I have."

"I know it sounds strange."

"No, it's not that it's strange. It's just that, I've never felt that way. I have felt like I wanted to be someplace else but that's about it."

Blaire nodded. "I'm starting to think that I'm off. That something is wrong. That I'm asleep and need to wake up."

Joanna touched her hand. "I'm your best friend. I want you to feel like you can come to me about anything. So it's okay to go into a little more detail if you want."

Blaire sighed long and hard. "I think I'm looking too deeply into things."

"We all are looking too deeply into things." She nudged her with a grin on her face. "I'm still thinking about the Strong Curls Benefit the other night. Whatever happened to Mr. Highest Bidder anyway?"

"I don't know. He just...he just disappeared."

"Has he tried to contact you again?"

"Nope."

Joanna packed the remainder of her sandwich away. "He seemed odd. Not that he isn't a charitable person and all, because I don't know him personally. But it seems he wanted you to see him. Like really *see* him."

"So why didn't he stay? Why give the date away?"

"I can't explain it. But I have a feeling you're going to find out soon."

Mason was driving down the road talking on his cell phone to his son Derrick. He sounded agitated which did nothing to Mason's already volatile mood. Especially since Dasher had enraged him beyond belief.

By T. Styles

"Are you listening, Pops?" He yelled. "Because I need fucking help right now."

Mason fell deeper into his seats and adjusted his smoke colored shades. "I hear you, son."

"So, what can I do? Because she acting like we don't have a family. She acting like she don't have to come home and it's fucked up."

"What do you want from her?"

"What that supposed to mean?"

"One minute you beefing and the next ya'll together." He shrugged. "So, I'm asking what you *really* want?"

"I want her to act right. And be a mother. She should be cooking and cleaning too, but she won't fall in line. I think she—."

"Derrick, you going about shit the wrong way. You can't force her to act right if she don't want to be with you."

"Who said she doesn't want to be with me? She told you that?"

He shook his head. "Nobody said that. I'm basing it on her actions." He pulled up into a lot and parked. "Now, I know you having trouble, but you have to ask yourself what you want from this girl. If you really want to be with her, then do everything you can to prove it."

"But what if she don't...I mean, what if she don't act right still? What if she tries to take my kid and I don't ever see him again?"

"First off that won't fucking happen."

"What if it does, Pops?"

"If she leaves you, then you have your answer. But it don't mean she get to take Patrick. We all know that." He delivered a veiled threat. "Listen, do I think Shay is made for you? Yes. But sometimes you have to let what's made for you walk away."

"Aight, Pops. I'm out."

When he ended the call, Mason peered around the parking lot from the inside of his vehicle. He nodded when he saw Blaire pull up in her Range with Joanna. Taking a deep breath, he pushed out and walked toward her.

The moment Blaire saw his face, she smiled and then cleared her throat trying not to appear too excited. He looked smooth in his designer blue jeans, black t-shirt and shades.

He knew he was a star.

"Uh, Joanna, I'll see you in a minute." She said as they piled out.

Joanna glared at Mason and looked back at her. "Are you sure?"

Blaire nodded and Joanna walked off.

Moving slowly toward Mason she crossed her arms. "Uh, if I remember correctly, you gave our date away. So why are you here?"

He nodded. "I know, but it was the right thing to do."

She grinned. "Is that correct?"

"Yep. While you were playing hostess on the podium, I had to listen to him go on and on about how you were so beautiful." He placed a hand over his heart. "And since I'm sorta like cupid, I figured I'd help him out and all."

She giggled and his heart jumped. "Cupid huh?"

"Yep."

She smiled brighter but then grew serious. "Why do I...I mean...why do I feel like we've met before?"

"We did. At the benefit."

"No, seriously. I feel like, I feel like I know you more than I know anybody else. And I, I don't understand. Did we meet?"

"Well if you knew me, you would remember me, right?"

"Not really." She said softly, not being able to tell him about her past.

"Why? You suffer from memory loss or something?" He was doing the most, but he needed to know. As he examined her closely, trying to figure out if she was faking, he got his answer. In that moment, it was obvious that she was clueless.

"No, I, I mean...it's hard to explain."

"I have time."

She shook her head. "I wouldn't feel comfortable bearing my soul to a stranger. No offense but, it's crazy that you even showed up to my job."

"I knew you were thinking about me." He laughed. "So, I had to bless you with a visit."

She giggled. "Oh really?"

"Yep, your eyes were lit when I walked across that room. Like you were on a nigga's dick and shit. So, I figured I would give you the benefit of the doubt and bless you with my presence."

She glared. "Wait, are you serious as you are gross?"

"As a heart attack."

She frowned. "That is the most arrogant shit I've ever heard in my life."

"Why is it arrogant when its facts?"

"You don't know me to say what's factual. Remember? We haven't met. To be honest I haven't given another thought about you."

"I doubt that." He crossed his arms over his chest and laughed once.

Blaire's face turned red. "Let me be clear, I don't ever want to see you here again. As a matter of fact, I never want to see you period."

"Wait, I was just play—."

"Get off my property! Before you are escorted off, Mr. Arrogant!"

When Joanna's last employee left her office, she got up from her desk and closed the door. Looking around to make sure no one was entering; she took a deep breath and made a call.

"I think she met someone from her past," she said, as she sat on the side of the desk while looking through her glass wall at the Strong Curls staff seated in cubicles.

Gina sighed. "How do you know?"

"He seemed confident and sure of himself when he approached. Almost as if he knew his presence would remind her of home."

"What is his name?"

Joanna looked down and then straight ahead. "I can't remember." She lied.

"I need you to find out who he is. Because if it's Mason Louisville, he can destroy everything I'm trying to build."

"But why?" Joanna asked honestly. "If he cares about her, maybe his presence will allow her to be happier. Because lately, lately she's been sad. And I'm concerned that—."

"Have you forgotten how this works?"

Silence.

"You have been in a sexual relationship with your step-father for over five years. And it's ongoing. Don't make me destroy your life, by letting everyone around you know you're fucking your mother's husband." She paused. "Now, find out if this mystery man is Mason Louisville. Because if it is, we have a lot of work to do."

Gina hung up and called her Butler through the intercom. When he entered her bedroom, she sighed. "Listen, I need you to get in touch with my sons Hercules and Aaron."

He stood in the doorway. "Is everything okay?"

"I'm just concerned that, well, I have some concerns that need addressing." She didn't feel like explaining herself to the help.

He shuffled a little. "Listen, if you want my assistance I—."

"Do what I ask!"

He raked his oily hair back roughly and looked at her with penetrating green eyes. "Yes, ma'am, right away."

Jersey was babysitting Patrick and her daughter when Dasher entered without an invitation. "What's going on?"

"Are you fucking Mason or something?" She asked, crossing her arms over her chest tightly. "Because he's mine now in case you didn't know."

Jersey's jaw dropped.

"Well?" Dasher threw her arms up. "Are you putting out or not?"

Jersey broke out into heavy laughter. "I have no idea what sparked your stupid ass to walk up in here like you crazy, but fucking Mason is the last of my worries. And if you were smart, they should be the first of your concerns. Because the nigga ain't shit."

"I'm not leaving him, Jersey. Don't ask me why, but I, I can't let him go. And you should be ready for a battle from me if you retaliate. I know I am." She walked out, rubbing her six-pack belly.

By T. Styles

Aaron and Hercules Petit walked through the foyer of the Petit Estate, after their mother summoned them. Propped in her wheelchair, looking like death connected to oxygen, she sat in the middle of the floor.

"You called?" Hercules said, scratching his grey curly hair.

"I need you to follow Blaire when she isn't here."

"Mother, you cut us off." Aaron said. The younger of the two, he was devastated the most when Gina chose to isolate them from the family funds and home.

"I didn't cut you off. I did however kick you out of my house. Because—."

"You're holding two people in the attic, mother and we said something about it!" Hercules yelled. "That's why you put us out. I was only expressing my concerns. That's it."

"And you are lying to your own grandchild about who *he* really is!" Aaron added.

"*She.*" She said through the mask. "Who *she* really is." She balled up a wrinkled fist.

The brothers looked at one another. There was no use in talking to her and they knew it.

"So, I take it you won't help me." Gina continued.

"What exactly do you want us to help you with, mother?" Hercules glared.

"I believe someone from Blaire's past has reentered the picture. And I need to make sure they don't get in our way. All I want for you to do is to follow her and let me know what you discover."

"Where is Officer Logan?" Aaron asked. "He usually does your dirty work."

"He's doing something else."

"I'm sorry, mother, but we can't do that." Hercules paused. "But what we *will* do is keep your secret. And for that you will restore our income to its weekly state. You're beyond wealthy now."

Gina glared. "And if I don't?"

"Then we will tell Banks everything he needs to know."

Marshall was next in line at the drive in ATM. There was a car ahead of him as he spoke to

By T. Styles

Hercules on the phone. He was a handsome man of Mexican descent in his thirties, who turned heads every time he walked into a room.

"I know you said not to call her but, I don't know, it's not fair how she uses people up. And personally, I don't trust her around young boys. Did she ever bother you? Sexually?"

Silence.

"Hercules?"

"My mother will get what's coming to her, Marshall. Of this I'm sure. I don't know how. And I don't know when. But you don't get to be as evil as she is and not reap what you sow. But you should not have threatened her by telling her what you know."

"You did though."

"I did because I'm her blood relative. She uses and disposes of everyone else. Now I look at you like you're family. We practically grew up together. Which is why I was willing to give you some of the money she gave to me recently. But threatening her, brother, is not good."

"What do you think I should do?"

"I think when she gives you the money, you should go back to Mexico. You can live like a king there. Her old age doesn't make her less deadly; it makes her worse."

"What is he doing!" Marshall said, about the car ahead of him, that didn't seem to be doing any business at the ATM.

"What's going on?"

"The car in front of me isn't moving."

"Get out of there, Marshall! It's probably Logan!"

"What are you talking about?" He joked, it's just a car with a rude ass—."

When a tall police officer exited the vehicle in front of him and stomped toward his window, his heart thumped.

"Marshall, what's going on, man? Talk to me!"

"I love you, Hercules. Give Aaron my love too."

BOOM!

The glass shattered and he was killed immediately.

CHAPTER SIX

Derrick had far too much to drink as he sat at the bar, eavesdropping on his girlfriend. He had been following her for nights and saw nothing of importance. And finally, he felt like he was close on solving the case.

He was watching her sitting with her hairdresser and a few friends having a good time which fucked him up mentally.

They hadn't spent quality time since Banks Wales was gone.

He had been watching for two hours. Even arrived at the bar before they had, due to hijacking her text messages earlier in the evening and finding out the location. He was trying to get one clue as to what was really going on with the woman he hated to admit that he loved.

Before the first drink she arrived at the bar uptight, and he wondered what was on her mind. But after some time, and a few more shots, she lit up like the Vegas skyline and appeared to become the life of the party.

While he felt like wet shit.

He despised himself for what he let her reduce him too. Afterall he was a Lou, and Louisville men didn't have to chase females. And yet that was exactly what he was doing. Because above all, he hated that she was losing interest.

"Girl, do you see that nigga over there," Shay's hairdresser said as she nudged Shay's arm.

Shay looked in the direction of the man but shook her head. "Nah. You know that's not my thing."

"Not your thing?" She laughed. "Bitch, are you crazy?"

"I'm not about to go over there and ask no man to talk to me. It ain't my speed so why play myself like it is?"

"That's my bitch," Derrick cheered to himself after hearing her refuse to take the dick bait.

All of the women laughed at her. "Why the fuck not?" Sandra, the hairdresser continued. It was like she was trying her best to separate them. "It ain't like Derrick been doing what he supposed to be doing in the bedroom."

"What the fuck?" Derrick said to himself.

"And it ain't like he been treating you right either." She continued.

"Girl, stop it." Shay waved the air. "You only know the half I tell you."

"And the half that you tell us is fucked up."

"It's true," Red Hair said. "If I were you, I wouldn't waste much more of my time on no Louisville nigga."

"Well, it ain't that easy to walk away." Shay took a sip of her drink. "If it was, I'd be gone already."

"Why ain't it easy though? Because if you ask me, it's simple. A man is over there giving you the eyes and you over here giving them to us instead."

"I'm not going to do it because, well, for starters, me and Derrick got a kid together and...and I don't want to fuck that up because of a maybe. A girl needs a protector. And for now, he's mine."

As they continued to talk, Derrick's anger level reached fever pitches. He never liked anybody outside of the family but hearing how they talked about him behind his back made him hate her friends even more.

To the point of feeling like he wanted to commit murder.

He was just about to go home and save the rest of his dignity when Shay, after a lot of pushing and another tequila shot, courtesy of her friend, walked over to the man.

The way the stranger's face lit up as the pretty girl with the long light brown braids strutted over to him caused Derrick to see black.

In fact, that was all he needed to act stupid.

As if he morphed from nowhere, he rushed up to Shay from across the bar, snatched her by the arm and yanked her outside. She didn't even know he was present.

Tucked in a nasty alley, he read her, her rights. "Fuck is your problem, huh?" He pointed at the bar with his free hand. "You supposed to be hanging out with them bitches, and you about to approach some nigga?"

"Get off me!" She snatched away.

He grabbed her back. "Bitch, don't tell me to get off you. Shit is dangerous out here. You supposed to be social distancing and—."

She snatched off again. "Nigga..." **Clap**. "What" **Clap**. "Do" **Clap**. "You" **Clap**. "Want?"

He pointed in her face. "Call me a nigga one more time and watch what the fuck I do. I'm begging you so I can go off."

She sighed deeply. "Derrick, why are you here? Really?"

92   By T. Styles

"I...I..." His spirit told him to say he missed her. His mind told him to plead with the part of her that he was certain was still in love. He wanted to tell her how he planned to try harder and be a better man. Instead he said, "I'm here because you have a son. And you don't need to be out here acting like no whore."

She shook her head and looked down. "And here I thought you missed me. I should have known that everybody who cared about me died a long time ago."

"Fuck that supposed to mean?"

"I'm alone, Derrick. My parents are dead. And my adopted parents are dead too. And you and your father don't give a fuck. I gotta know were Banks is! I gotta know if he's okay! He's all I have left."

"Don't tell me how I feel, Shay."

"Oh, so you been looking for Banks like I been asking? Like I been begging?"

"I mean...we been asking around and..."

"Asking around? I need you to comb the streets. I need you to do what you would if Mason was missing. I bet you'd tear up the east coast then."

"Shay, he's gone-gone. Preach said it and if it weren't true my father would have let me know. You gotta let Banks go."

"But I can't!" She cried. "And what about that Nasty Natty bitch who wants to fuck you? She was the last one seen with Minnesota and Spacey. If you find her, maybe we can find them and then we can find Banks. Because I feel like them all going missing at the same time is connected."

"I tried already." He pointed at himself. "I'm the one who found out they found Natty's Benz in the river, remember? So, if you ask me, she's dead too."

"Nah, what I'm just finding out is that you don't give a fuck about nobody but yourself, Derrick. And I'm—."

He kissed her roughly.

At first, she fought back, even wiggled away a little. But after a few more seconds her body relaxed as her back pressed against the grungy brick wall. Before she knew what was happening, he lifted her up so that her legs could drape around the sides of his hips.

Back and forth he pushed into her moist pussy, until she was filled with so much dick, her lower stomach ached.

94   By T. Styles

In and out he pumped until he exploded into her body. He couldn't even last. It was a few seconds before she reached an orgasm too.

When he was done, he put her down and looked at her. "That's all your ass needed huh?" He fastened his pants. "Some dick."

She giggled and wiped her braids out of her face. "You stupid."

"You need to relax, Shay." He said softly, hoping they were over the dumb shit and could grab something to eat. "Things will work out. Okay?" He buckled his belt.

She nodded. "Okay." She pulled her dress down and kissed him on the cheek. "I'll see you at home later."

"At home later?" He glared. "Ain't you coming with me?"

"Nah, I'm still chilling with my friends." With that she walked away.

Instead of getting in his car, from the window he watched his girl be welcomed back into the opening arms of her funky ass friends. This after he dicked her down in the alley like a tramp.

For some reason, at the moment, he felt stupid. Soft. Having pleasured her with nothing but a nut in it for him. It was like she played his heart, took the dick and gave no fucks.

Back in the day when they had sex after a fight, they would grab something to eat and talk about how stupid it was to waste so much time beefing.

But now things were different.

As he watched her with her friends, the hairdresser happened to catch him staring from the window.

He gave her a look of evil before nodding and walking away.

Blaire was leaving her building when Mason approached her from behind. "Excuse me, can I have five minutes?"

"Didn't I tell you to stay away from me?"

"Yes but, look, I hated how I came off and I want another chance to—."

"I don't give out second chances, sir."

"Just hear me out, Blaire." He said with an extended hand which landed on his heart. "I know I messed up. I came off harsh and wrong. But I'm a good person."

"People who say they are good people often are not."

"That may be true for some. And I definitely don't want to imply I don't have struggles in the personality department. But I have all intentions on doing right by you. By respecting you. And I'm asking for a chance. Just, just think about it. Don't say anything else. And maybe when the time is right, I'll see you again."

He walked away.

Walid was in the kitchen going into the refrigerator. The plan was to grab some cookie dough and chomp on it with Ace in their room, who was too busy watching movies in their theater to take the trip.

He had successfully located the chocolate chip cookie batter when Frances walked into the kitchen. Grabbing him by his little wrist she said, "You aren't supposed to be in here."

"Get off me!" He snatched away.

"Who do you think you're talking to little—."

Suddenly Frances was yanked by the back of her uniform by Blaire as Walid grinned.

"What exactly are you doing touching my son like that?"

"He was...I was..."

"If I ever catch you grabbing him like that again, there will be trouble. Am I understood?"

Silence.

"Am I understood?" Blaire moved closer, hovering over her much shorter frame.

Frances straightened her dress abruptly and panted. "Yes." She paused. "Will there be anything else?"

Both Blaire and Walid said, "Nah."

CHAPTER SEVEN

After making sure her grandson and her daughter were sound asleep, Jersey grabbed her cell phone and baby monitor. Ready to have a little fun, she crept to one of the guestrooms. Sitting on the bed, she adjusted her pillows. Next, she looked at her face on video, smoothed a few loose hairs with a wet finger from her mouth, and made the Facetime call.

"Wow, I didn't think you would hit me back tonight," Perry said when he saw her pretty face on the screen.

"Why would you say that?" She grinned. "Because for real I've been thinking of you all night."

He chuckled. "For starters we were just getting into it when you had to bounce. I thought I was gonna see that pink pussy straight up, but you cut me off. My dick was rock hard too."

She sighed and wiped her hair out of her face. "I know shit tight right now. I mean, it's one of the reasons I wasn't sure if we could do this when I met you online."

"Do what?"

"You know, the long-distance relationship thing. I mean, I like you a lot Perry. I do. But I have kids. I'm older than you and—."

"You know age doesn't matter to me."

"But it matters to me."

"Listen, I promise not to bring up what you do when we aren't together if you promise not to keep talking to me about age. Deal?"

"Deal." She giggled. "Now show me that dick."

"So, you just want to jump right back in, huh? Don't wanna warm a nigga up with nasty talk or nothing?"

"You know it. I—." When her phone beeped, she looked at the caller's name. Her heart rate kicked up. "Perry, I'm sorry but I have to go."

"Go?" He frowned. "But you just hit me back."

"I know and I really apologize. An important business call I've been waiting on just came through. I'll hit you when I'm done."

"Whatever, Jersey."

"Please don't be mad at me. I—."

The screen went black.

She had no time for his fluttering heart. There was work to do. Cases to solve.

Jersey quickly called back Detective Tim Luther. "Have you found out anything about

By T. Styles

Banks? Or Howard? Or...or, Preach?" She was anxious and on edge.

"I prefer to talk in person."

She rolled her eyes. "Let me guess, you need more money."

"Surveillance is expensive work, Mrs. Louisville. But I'm good at my job. Now if you don't want my help, I understand but—."

"Meet me here in an hour."

"I'll be there in thirty minutes."

As she rushed to her room to put on something more presentable, she was surprised to see Mason entering the mansion with an attitude. "What's wrong with you? Fighting Dasher again?" The plan was to tell him how she approached her the other day, but she wanted to see if he knew first.

"Nah."

"Mason, I know we aren't together but—."

"How come you do that? Whenever we talk you always gotta bring up the fact that we not together. I know that shit, and I'm good with it too."

"I didn't think it was a problem. I just want you to know that we can still talk."

"It's not a problem but it is annoying as fuck."

She sighed. "You know what, it doesn't even matter. But have you...you know, found out anything about our son?"

He frowned. "No, and you know if I had I would tell you."

"Well what about Banks? And Preach?"

He shook his head. "No. I didn't. But—."

DING DONG...

He turned around to look at the massive door. "Who that?"

"A private investigator."

His eyes bulged. "For fucking what?"

She opened the door and the investigator walked inside. He had a different physique than what most believed investigators should look like. He was young, fit and white with piercing blue eyes. He also had a sense of fashion, choosing to wear designer jeans, a soft white t-shirt and a soft blue surgical face mask.

"I thought you said thirty minutes." Jersey said.

"I was in the neighborhood."

"What is this, Jersey?" Mason glared.

Tim extended his hand, but Mason didn't bother to shake it. "Okay..." Tim said pulling down his mask and backing up a few feet to social distance and all.

"What is this about?" Mason asked.

The detective dropped his hand and cleared his throat. Before talking, he looked at Jersey and she nodded in approval. "Well, I was hired to find a Banks Wales, Howard Louisville and..." he looked down at his notes. "I believe his name is Preach." He looked up at Mason.

"Banks Wales?" Mason yelled. "Fuck for?"

Jersey found his statement odd. "He said all those names and that's the only person you can say?"

"I want to know what the fuck he looking for all of them for. Preach left town, Howard ran off because of family issues and Banks is dead. Case closed! Now pay the man!"

Truthfully no one knew where Preach was, and it bothered Mason greatly. Mainly because after locating Banks, he knew Preach told him a lie when he said Banks died due to the botched brain surgery they all facilitated. So, his intentions were to murder him on sight. But Preach skipped town.

Jersey stepped closer. "Well, I don't believe he's dead and—."

"I told you I would handle this shit!"

"But you haven't!" She yelled.

Mason walked toward the door and opened it wider. "You know what, just get out, man."

"Mason, you can't do that. I invited him here!"

"This is my fucking house and I want this white boy gone."

The investigator looked at Jersey and sighed. "You know how to reach me, Mrs. Louisville."

When he left, she sighed. "You should not have done that."

"Stay out of this shit!"

"You should know that Banks left me well off, Mason. Financially, I have enough money to find out everything I need to know. Trust me."

"Yeah, aight." He walked away.

When he was gone, she hit the detective back on her cell phone. "Don't go too far. Meet me a mile up so we can talk."

CHAPTER EIGHT

Blaire walked through the door of her home, only to see Gina on the floor in agony. She had fallen out of her chair and was moaning in pain. Afraid for her well-being, she dropped her suitcase and ran to help her up.

"Grandmother, what...what happened?" She examined her body with her eyes quickly.

"Oh, I'm fine." She waved the air. "The nurse just left, and I couldn't catch her to tell her I fell."

Blaire placed the oxygen mask over her face and pulled the chair in front of her before helping her up. "Don't tell me you're fine. This is the third time this month you were on the floor. Where is Carl? And Frances? They should be helping you!"

"It's fine." She sighed. "No need to make a big deal about me all of the time. Old is old and it was bound to happen."

"Old is old?" She yelled. "You could've died!"

"But I didn't."

"Grandmother!"

"Blaire, I have no intentions on dying while lying on the floor." She sighed long and hard. "My death story will be far more creative than that."

"You know what, I'm going to take a leave of absence. That way I can look after you while you—."

"No."

"No what?"

"No, I don't want you doing that, Blaire. I want you to…continue to work on what we've built. That is more important than everything else."

"Grandmother, I have hired a very competent group. Who can run Strong Curls while I stay with you and—."

"Listen, we've come so far. I need to know that when I'm gone things will be as we want them to be. As we dreamed."

"What good is it if you die and—."

"I *am* going to die, Blaire. And I'm going to die soon. But when I'm gone, I'll take comfort in knowing that we built something together. You and I." She put a soft wrinkled hand on her face. "And don't let Aaron and Hercules change anything. It's my dying wish."

Blaire got the shivers. "I hate to talk about stuff like that." She sighed.

"Death is normal."

"I get it but you, you are the only person I have in my life outside of the twins. If something were

By T. Styles

to happen to you, I honestly don't believe I'll be able to make it. And I...I need to have you around, grandmother."

Gina could sense her anxiousness. "I get it."

"So, what about my uncles? Should we call them at least?"

Gina glared and rolled away from Blaire. Sitting in front of the bar she poured herself a drink. "I don't want them here."

"Why?"

"Because there are things you don't know about them."

"Things like what?" She threw her hands up. "Because to be honest, I'm tired of all the secrecy. What is it about my uncles that bothers you so much? I've only seen them twice that I can remember."

"Let's just say that some people work for the things they have, and others believe that because their house is built on gold, they don't have to mine for it. And I'm tired of dragging them along."

"So, this is about money then?"

"It's always about money when you're wealthy."

"Not for me."

Gina poured two glasses of whiskey and gave Blaire a drink. "I know. Which is why you run my business and not them. When we, when we made the shift from the cancer hair serum to African American hair care products, not everyone was on board."

"So, this is about me being black too?"

"No, I mean, it's about you being different."

"And the only way I'm different is because I'm black." She took a sip.

"It's not that simple. I know it may seem like it is, but Hercules and Aaron are, well, used to things going down a different path. They had plans for the business that didn't meet mine. And that's okay too."

Blaire took another much larger sip of whiskey and the moment she did, Mason's face flashed into her mind. As if the whiskey brought about a direct connection to him. Confused, her eyes widened, and she dropped the glass. Mainly because the vision she had was not based on a scenery she could recognize. She'd only seen him at the gala and in the parking lot. But in the memory flash she saw him in a house she couldn't picture.

"What's wrong, Blaire?"

Silence.

"Blaire, what's wrong?"

Slowly she turned toward Gina. "I'm not sure, and I don't understand why, but I...I think I just had a flashback."

A few minutes later, after putting Gina to sleep, Blaire realized Gina's skin was cold to the touch despite the temperature being comfortable throughout the mansion. Luckily the butler and the maid were in the room with her and seeing to her needs, so Blaire decided to check the house for some warmer blankets.

Before she knew it, she was at the highest part of the mansion, somewhere she had to admit, for whatever reason, she didn't roam. After catching the elevator upward, and locating the winter linen closet, she was about to grab a thicker blanket when she heard what sounded like voices behind a closed door.

It resembled a female and a male.

Curious, since the butler and the maid were downstairs, she was about to knock on the door when the Butler rushed up behind her. "Ma'am, can I help you with anything?"

"Uh, is someone in there?" She pointed at the door. "Do we have guests? I thought I heard—."

"No. It's empty." He said in a low voice.

Blaire frowned. "But I heard—."

"Trust me, you didn't hear anything."

Blaire was put off by his forwardness. Maybe she was hearing things since she also just saw a weird flashback.

"Did you want me to take the blanket to your grandmother?" He smiled awkwardly. "She's up again."

"Yes." She looked at the door once more.

"Sure, ma'am, can you come with me?" He placed a hand on her shoulder, leading her to the elevator. "Because I'm sure Mrs. Petit would love to see you again before she lays down for the night. You are her favorite girl."

Blaire had her workout gear on, which always included long sleeves. She was lacing up her sneakers when Joanna came over. After the butler announced her presence, Blaire stood up. "The treadmill is broken in our gym."

"Again?" Joanna said tossing her towel over her shoulder in frustration. "I was hoping to get a good workout in today."

"Yeah, I just told Carl to order another one. Should be here tomorrow."

"Dang, I was really looking forward to sweating it out." Joanna pouted.

"Me too." Blaire paused. "I figured we can find a nice park since the gyms are still closed."

"What about jogging around the mansion?" Joanna suggested. "It's a beautiful day and we've never done it before."

Blaire took a moment to think about the idea. Once again, she was surprised that since she could remember, she hadn't bothered to walk the lands of her own property. It was almost like she was programmed not to roam, like a baby elephant tethered to a tree. Who even as an adult, forgot how strong he was and so he remained.

"Sure, lets, let's do that."

Blaire and Joanna jogged around the mansion, while doing the regular which included talking about life at Strong Curls and beyond and in Joanna's case, men.

"I popped up over his house the other day," Joanna said, in short choppy words due to running. "I couldn't be without him. And he...he wasn't happy to see me."

"You mean after he hunted you down for days, he still wasn't happy?"

"No. I guess playing hard to get doesn't work for me. I should've accepted him back after he cheated and begged."

"Well did he know you were coming?"

"How could he know I was coming if I popped up," she giggled as her tennis shoes slammed into the grass. "Actually, he had another woman at his house."

"Wow, Joanna. I'm sorry."

"I know. I really made myself look desperate." She shook her head. "I'm really going to consider

By T. Styles

dealing with women because I can't be bothered with men anymore."

"Dealing with women?" Blaire frowned. "Is that something you've done before?"

"A few times in high school." She shrugged and looked over at Blaire. "Have you?"

Blaire couldn't remember anything about her past. "No, at least I don't think so."

"Well, are you attracted to women?"

"I definitely find women attractive. Meaning I know a beautiful woman when I see one."

Joanna nodded as they continued to jog. "Well would you...um...would you rule it out?"

Blaire laughed. "Joanna, are you making an offer?"

Silence.

Blaire was suddenly stunned as a cloud of awkwardness hung over their heads. In sync, they ran faster as if trying to escape the weird vibe.

"Um, any word about the generous stranger?" Joanna asked, doing her best to shift the subject.

"Not since he popped up for the second time." She shook her head. "He's very arrogant and yet there's something about him that feels familiar."

"He is good looking. I'll give him that."

"I guess so. But I don't think that's what moves me. It's almost like, well, he feels like a relative to me but different."

She nodded. "Did he say he knew you?"

"No...he definitely was introducing himself for the first time at the gala."

"I think you should be careful. You're worth a lot of money and sometimes people will show up hoping to take advantage. With secret agendas. Don't let him trick you. Wouldn't want to find you in the trunk of someone else's car."

"Someone else's car?"

Minnesota was looking out the window while Spacey was in the bathroom. Although he didn't like the window open, she enjoyed stealing views of the lawn when he wasn't around, because it relaxed her mood. She just saw two beautiful women jogging, one white and the other light skin and she wondered who they were. Something about the light skin woman drew her attention and she was just about to investigate harder when Spacey walked out.

"Thought we agreed to keep the window closed."

She shut it quickly. "Uh, yeah, you right." She paused. "Are you ready?"

He walked in front of her. "Yeah. I guess."

Minnesota examined him closely. "Okay, try it now, but remember to keep your eyes lowered."

"This is so stupid."

"It is, but if you don't try, we will never be able to get out of the attic, Spacey. You have to put everything you can into this. Please." She touched his arm. "So, when she calls on you again, if she will, you'll be ready."

"How do you know this will even work? Just because I try to be submissive or whatever, doesn't mean that bitch will let us go. We've done this before."

"I feel like she's testing us. I mean, based on the book grandmother left in the walls, why else would she keep us here? She wants us to be weakened. Physically and emotionally."

"She wants something that's for sure." He thought about his time with Gina. "Maybe you're the one who's supposed to be leaving."

"Spacey, don't..."

"I'm serious." He paused. "What if you're the only person who is supposed to get out of here? What if I'm supposed to...what if I'm supposed to die?"

"I don't want to hear you talk like..." Suddenly Minnesota fell out on the floor.

"Minnie!" His eyes widened in fear. "Minnie!"

Silence.

He picked her up and placed her on his bed since it was closest. It took everything out of him too. Breathing heavily, he said, "Minnie, are you okay?"

"Minnesota," she said softly, correcting him on her name.

"I don't care about all that. What's wrong?"

"I feel...I feel light-headed."

He thought about a few things. He'd been through this many times before. "It's your cycle again?"

"I think so...I feel, I feel wet between my legs."

Minnesota always had problematic menstrual cycles, but lately it had gotten so bad, she would

By T. Styles

be too weak to walk the first two days of her period. A few times they were certain she would die and even attempted to use the concern as a reason to leave the attic. But when Gina sent a doctor who assured her that Minnesota would be okay with rest, their hopes of getting free were put away.

"Oh shit, I see blood." Spacey said as he looked down at her white cotton pajama pants. "Can you walk to the bathroom?"

"No." She closed her eyes. "I'm too...too weak."

He stood up and paced in place.

He could barely walk most days without taking a breath himself, so carrying her to the bathroom would pull everything out of him. Having to change her was something he wasn't interested in doing either. He even considered picking her up and putting her on her own bed, but that would be just wrong. She would still need his help like in the past.

He was just about to try to lift her up when he heard a sound at the door. The noise was low, as if it were coming from the floor. Slowly he walked toward it, got on his hands and knees and looked under the doorway.

When he did, he saw small eyes staring back at him.

"Hello." Spacey said.

"Hello." The little voice responded.

"Who are you?"

"Walid."

Spacey's heartbeat kicked up. The little one on the other side of the door was his brother. Whom he held as a child but hadn't seen in years. He always believed the twins were in the house but now he was given proof.

"Walid, I remember you."

"You do?"

"Yes...I'm your big brother."

"So why are you in 'dere?"

Spacey laughed at his cute little voice. "I'm here because someone wants to keep me away. They don't want me to get out. Maybe you can help me."

"Okay...wait one minute." Footsteps trailed away from the door.

When he heard the elevator opening and closing, Spacey stood up and smiled. Walid coming to visit was the best part in a long time, and then he realized he probably should have warned him against telling Gina. The last thing he needed was her stopping him from coming.

When he looked back over at Minnesota, he remembered he hadn't cleaned her up yet. The

By T. Styles

moment he rose, he felt dizzy and leaned against the door for support. When he got his bearings together, he went to the bathroom and grabbed a washcloth with warm water. Next he removed Minnesota's soiled pants and underwear.

Blood was everywhere.

He quickly dipped the cloth into the water and began washing her inner thighs, and when they were cleaned, he dunked the water again and washed between her legs. She smelled of iron. Moving her vagina lips aside to get it good, he was trying to be careful.

But since he was touching a woman, his body heated, and he hated the sensation that was trying to take over. Within seconds, his dick was stiff and hard.

"Are you okay?" She asked touching his leg.

He jumped. Her eyes were closed so he hadn't realized she was conscious. "I'm, I'm fine."

"Thank you for doing this." She smiled although gravely embarrassed.

He nodded. "Next time pass out on your side of the room. Or in the bathroom."

She giggled. "Thank you."

When he was done washing her up, he changed her clothing and carried her to her bed. Then he changed his sheets and flopped on his bed, while looking at her as she was lying on her side.

"What you smiling at?" She asked, barely able to keep her eyes open.

He shook his head. "Nothing at all."

"It was nasty huh?"

"The grossest thing I've ever seen in my life."

"I know. I hate that I get so weak during this time of the month. And I don't know why it's getting worse."

"You lost a lot of blood too. Doesn't seem natural."

"Well the doctor said my iron levels are fine."

"How do we know we can trust them though?"

"We don't." She yawned. "But what other choice do I have?"

"None." They both said at the same time.

"So, you want me to ask the doctor to come back and—"

Suddenly cookie dough came sliding across the floor like a hockey puck from under the door. Minnesota jumped in fright but quickly laid back down due to feeling dizzy. "What is that?"

He smiled. "I forgot to tell you. That's our little brother. It's Walid."

By T. Styles

CHAPTER NINE

Blaire stood in the mirror, wearing only her panties. On the table next to her sat a glass of whiskey, which she needed most nights when she looked at her body's reflection. She couldn't say she hated herself. But she did feel as if what she saw, didn't represent who she felt like inside.

Running her hand over her flat chest, she sighed deeply. Her breasts had been removed and she wondered what happened in her life to warrant such a violent operation. The removal forced her frame into masculinity, which oddly enough, didn't bother her in the least.

Who needed such wobbly things anyway?

Since Blaire had no idea that in the past, she was transgender, she also didn't know Gina had done everything in her power to shield this fact. Including having her tattoos removed while she was unconscious and scheduling her for a breast enhancement. But Blaire declined the elective surgery, promising to do it later in the year.

As of the moment, no date had been scheduled.

Sighing deeply, she put on her A size silicone breast that was formed to fit her body, along with her matching black bra. Afterwards she slipped on a beautiful black dress with light crystals throughout. When she was done, she blew out her long curly hair and added a bit of makeup which she always hated. But grandmother told her even Picasso used paint.

When there was a knock at the door she said, "Come in."

Gina rolled inside and parked her wheelchair near the doorway. Blaire often wondered if she was stronger than she let on sometimes.

"Blaire, you look beautiful."

She shook her head. "You're biased." She giggled.

"I'm serious. I feel so proud to call you my granddaughter."

Blaire turned around, only to see a set of pearls in Gina's hand. "Wear these for me tonight, Please."

Her eyes widened. "But those are your favorite."

"I know. Which is why I want you to have them."

Blaire walked over and softly removed them from her hand before placing them around her neck. "Wow, these are...these are amazing."

They weren't.

By T. Styles

"They look perfect on you." She sighed.

Blaire walked over to the mirror and observed herself. The pearls made her look more feminine, which suited the look but not her heart. "Grandmother, why is the attic off limits?"

Gina blinked a few times. She hadn't expected such a silly, crazy question. "Off limits?" She said softly. "Honey, nothing is off limits to you in this house."

"Well it feels that way. I've tried several times to access that attic, only to be stopped by either Carl or Frances. It's as if they are safeguarding what's inside. So, what's inside?"

"That isn't true, dear. No one is guarding anything."

"I could've sworn I heard voices behind that door, grandmother."

"Voices?" She laughed. "Honey, you sound like me. This house has a way of echoing. But there is no one living in this home besides you, me, and the twins." She sighed. "And of course, Frances and Carl when they're on duty."

"I would like to see what's there."

Gina was concerned. Blaire had been so trained that she didn't think she would ever ask. She would have to make a decision on killing one if not both of her children soon.

They could no longer remain in the garret.

"Blaire, I...well, I didn't want to tell you this but, well, I have some painful memories up there. Memories of a time when my people suffered great atrocities in France."

"Why?" She frowned.

"Blaire, what I'm saying is, well, my family was persecuted because of our desire to flee to America."

"Seems like a silly reason to persecute anyone."

"True. But it was a painful period where there were better opportunities here. So, I've been keeping keepsakes of those times in the attic. To preserve the past while not letting it impact the present."

"Oh...I see."

"If there was anything I thought would give you a sense of your past, I would take you up there myself. It is my private space and I need you to respect that."

Blaire nodded. "Understood."

She needed to skip the subject, believing Blaire's antennas were raising too high. "Oh, uh,

Blaire, I think we need to get Walid a little more care."

She frowned. "Why, why do you say that?"

"He doesn't seem, well, he seems off a little."

Blaire folded her arms. "Is he getting into the refrigerator again? Because I told him not to go into the kitchen but there something about that white flour that he loves to play with. I don't know—."

"No, it's not that. He, well, lies. You can't believe everything he says because of it." She stuttered trying to cling to one lie. "And I'm afraid if we don't get him help, he might rub off on Ace's gentle heart."

"Wow, it's that bad?"

"Yes. We really need to be careful and address those issues now, before he gets out of hand."

Blaire nodded. "Yeah, maybe you're, maybe you're right."

Shay's hairdresser was in her salon, looking at dick pictures with a few of her employees. Between the three of them, they collected different pics along with profile pics for their amusement of the men they fucked over their lifetimes. It was something they took seriously. Like a club even.

There was one caveat. To prove you really had the dick in question, you actually had to be holding the dick with a familiar ring. And Amy did just that.

"Girl, I can't believe you had that nigga's shit in your mouth!" Sandra said laughing.

"Not only did I have it in my mouth, I kept it there for a long time too, because he kept hollering about how good it felt between my lips." She giggled. "It was the sweetest thing I tasted in a long time."

"Well give us details before one of our clients gets here and ruins shit." Sandra said, rubbing her hands together.

Amy grinned. "Okay, he..." She stopped talking and looked out the window. "Wait, ain't that Shay's dude?"

Everyone turned to the window in the front of the shop. "It sure is, with his fine ass." Sandra said.

By T. Styles

"Well I wonder what he's doing here?"

"Guess we're about to find out."

Derrick opened the door and the bells dinged. "Aye, Sandra, can I holla at you for a second?"

"Okay, but you know you supposed to wear a mask, right?" She pointed to a sign on the wall that was hanging on by a thread. Tilted and everything.

"I ain't got nothing." He winked. "You can trust me."

She didn't give a fuck for real about no virus. None of her employees did for that matter. She just liked giving people a hard time, calling it foreplay. "Okay, meet me outside."

When he left Amy said, "Don't forget the ring."

Sandra wiggled her ass and bopped out the door.

Five minutes later Derrick was driving Sandra around, as they smoked weed in his Benz truck. She was heavily flirtatious, which to him, was to be expected. "So, you really have never been to Hedonism?"

"Nah…"

"You missing out. Me and my friends go every year. Get the all-inclusive package at the resort and everything." She inhaled the blunt. "It's seriously the best thing you can ever do if you are into having a good time. Or if you're into voyeurism."

"So that's what they call freak shit now? Voyeurism?"

She frowned. "Somebody sounds a little judgmental."

"Nah, I just be wondering how people get down with having sex with folks they don't know in public."

"So, you never fucked a stranger?"

"Nah…never."

"Never met a person on the side of the road and said, I want this person to suck my dick?"

"I said nah." He shook his head while laughing.

"Well I do get my pussy ate by whoever is willing to lick it." She said proudly, as if she received a degree in Hoeism. "At least once a month."

"What is it about that shit that moves you?"

She sighed. "It breaks me out of my boring ass life. I mean, you get tired of doing the same thing over and over. So fucking strangers is new and fresh. It gives me life. More than doing hair."

"So how you gonna move now, that the world has changed? With the virus and all?"

She waved the air. "Fuck all that. I'm gonna die anyway right? If I die, I rather be somewhere getting dick."

He nodded. "You know what, I think I want to try it."

"Try what?"

"The fucking out in public shit you be talking about."

"I don't think I said out in public, but I hear you."

"You did say in public. Hedonism remember?"

"Yeah but—."

"Listen, I'm trying to fuck." He grew serious. "Are you with it or not?"

Fifteen minutes later they were in a park, within the densest portion. Horny above all else, Sandra was quickly taking her clothing off and adjusting her ring for the picture she planned to take for her friends for bragging rights, after she fucked him of course. She was halfway undressed when she realized he hadn't removed one shoe.

"You gotta move quick in case somebody comes." She tossed her pants on the ground and used it as a pad for her knees. "Hurry up."

"I was right." He glared down at her.

"About what?" She grinned touching his leg, like a dog begging for a treat.

"You a fucking whore."

Her eyes widened. "Wait, what is this?"

"Stay away from my girl."

"What is this about, Derrick?"

She glared and moved to get up until he said, "Stay the fuck down there where you belong. Before I hurt you."

She obeyed. "What do you want? I mean, I thought we were going to have a good time but now I see it's all a game."

"If I catch you around Shay again, I will kill you. Do you understand me?"

"You really shouldn't be threatening me."

By T. Styles

"But I am though. I started to tuck you in the ground when you jumped into my car. To be done with you all together. But now I realize you're not worth the case. So, I want you to stay away from her. Or I will come back and find you. Do you understand?"

Silence.

He moved his hand toward the back of his jeans, close to his .45 that he kept near. It was on the ready. "Do you understand, bitch?"

She nodded yes.

He grinned and removed his phone to snap a picture. "Good. Now find your own fucking way home."

When he walked away, Sandra made a call. "Gina, it's me, Sandra."

"What is it, girl?" She sighed.

"I've been doing as you've asked. Hanging with Shay and making sure they aren't talking about Banks."

"And?"

"Well Shay is fine, but her boyfriend is causing trouble. He just told me that he is still looking for Banks."

"Why are you with the boy?"

She looked down at her naked body. "Because he was just coming onto me. I wasn't interested but I did—."

"You were being a whore to get information. It's the oldest trick in the book." She sighed.

"Will you put the money in the account? I didn't get my check this week."

"I'll take care of you. Officer Logan will bring your money by personally."

When Gina got off the phone, she called the officer. "I need you to take out everyone in the Louisville family tonight. And the hairdresser too."

"I can't do it tonight. I'm at a benefit for officers and—."

"Well do it before the week ends. It's important. And it's also what you're being paid to do."

By T. Styles

CHAPTER TEN

Escorted in a black Mercedes E Class, Blaire arrived at Estate Gardens, a private restaurant for the wealthy. It was for her scheduled date from the auction. It was apparent Todd was intent on making the grounds beautiful because the scenery was magical.

The trees were covered in white Christmas style lights, along with the walkway for her arrival. When they drove up the long driveway, and parked in the front, Blaire's bodyguard opened the door to let her out just as Todd appeared at the opened door.

He was dressed in a navy-blue suit, red tie, giving a presidential look. A republican at that. "Wow, you look beautiful." He said.

Blaire smiled, although secretly she hoped that when she arrived, Mason would be there, waiting to greet her. And yet she wondered why she thought of him, since he was obviously so fucking arrogant.

"You look very handsome."

He extended his hand for hers. "Thank you. Come with me."

As they walked through the lavish establishment, outlined with gold, burgundy and pearl colors, they were escorted to a lone table in the back. Soft jazz music played in the air. Although they were indoors, the roof was opened, showcasing the beautiful stars above.

This scene seemed familiar.

Could it be another blast from the past?

After pulling out the chair for Blaire, Todd sat in his seat and looked over at her. "Wow, I've been waiting for this night for a very long time."

She nodded. "You earned it."

"Actually, I didn't." His head rose high. "Which brings me to my next point." He reached into his jacket and pulled out an envelope before sliding it across the table with a heavy index finger. "I never officially made a donation."

She smiled and opened the envelope. It was five hundred thousand dollars to be exact. "Thank you. This is very, very generous."

"No problem." He waved the air. "I got my allowance and..." He shook his head, after realizing he was embarrassed about being kept on a money leash. "Well, I mean, I got, well, I got my money." He cleared his throat. "I sound stupid, don't I?"

"No, you don't. I understand money is often funneled through appropriate channels. So, this is very generous. Like I said, this will help the foundation greatly."

He nodded. "Good because I really wanted to talk to you about something else too." Blaire sat back in her seat. But the sit back was different, masculine, and it put Todd off. "Sometimes you, you act differently."

"How so?"

"I can't explain it. I mean, don't get me wrong. You're a very beautiful woman but sometimes you, I don't know, seem mannish."

She glared and sat up straight, desperately in search for her femininity again. Touching her pearls, she said, "Well that's an insult."

"I'm not trying to be rude." He extended a palm in her direction. "I just wondered if you maybe ever played baseball or anything? Because you are tall."

"No, I never played."

"Well whatever it is, I like it. A lot."

As she sat across from him, trying to remain feminine at all times, she was again surprised at the effort he put into making things so nice as the waiter entered and exited with their meals. She didn't know what she expected, but it definitely wasn't this much effort.

"So, you were going to say something else..." Blaire said as the main course arrived, along with bread rolls so fresh they left pleasant odors in the air. "...before the manly comment."

"Oh yes," he laughed. "I was thinking that I know you believe I'm a kid. And I am younger than you. But I have plans. I have dreams."

"I don't doubt that."

"So, I was wondering if maybe, maybe this could be the beginning instead of an end. Because we both know I've been trying for a long time to take you out. To show you that I'm interested in taking a step further. Despite—."

"Todd, I can never look at you in that way."

"W...why not?"

"First off I'm well in my forties...I think."

"You think?"

"I believe I am. And, well, I wouldn't want you to waste your life on me when yours is just beginning."

He glared. Long and hard. "So, I did all of this for nothing?"

"Did all of what exactly?" She smiled while trying not to be rude. "Someone else donated a million dollars to—."

"I'm not talking about that stupid shit." He pounded a fist onto the table, rattling the lettuce within the bowl. "I'm talking about all of this." He looked around as if he owned the place.

She laughed. "So, you thought this alone was enough to impress me into being with you? Young man, I'm a billionaire. Who has access to every dollar in my account. I had a party for my children here. Relax."

"You don't want to make an enemy out of me." He lowered his brow. "I promise you don't."

It had been less than thirty minutes and already his true colors had shone through. And it was dirty brown.

Taking a deep breath, she swiped his check across the table and smiled. "You keep daddy's money. It's obvious you need it more than me." She got up from the table and he followed.

Grabbing her by the arm he said, "Don't walk away from—."

Suddenly his words were chopped when Blaire grabbed his throat, stopping oxygen flow. What scared her was not that his face was reddening, and he was losing air, but how easily she seemed to do the act.

She'd done this before she was certain.

When his lips were turning blue, she released him and ran out of the restaurant. "You'll pay for that!" He yelled from the floor. "Do you hear me? You'll pay!" He rolled to his hands and knees like a teacup Yorkie and coughed out a few breaths.

Once outside, when the cool air brushed against her face, she was shocked to see Mason was leaning on his car smiling. The plan was to apologize again for how he treated her at Strong Curls, but his smile washed away when he realized something was wrong.

"Banks, you good?" He asked rushing up to her.

"Banks?" She said softly. "Who is...who is Banks?"

Immediately, but much too late, he realized his error. "I mean Blaire. Is everything okay?"

Her eyes widened. Banks sounded so familiar. So personal.

So real.

"Who is...who is Banks?"

"Nobody. I was thinking about something else. Are you okay though?"

She shook her head no. "I don't think so."

"Well, come with me."

Derrick cruised in his car while talking to a friend of his on the phone. In the past he wasn't one for entertaining, but since his father was doing his thing, his mother had the baby and his brothers were dead, he longed for companionship, even if he didn't know it.

It didn't help matters that Shay was distant, and there was nothing he could do about it. And at the same time, he was sure that the hairdresser would tell Shay about their interaction, which would force her to be jealous and want him more.

He was so excited he couldn't wait.

"Nah, I haven't been to that strip club," Derrick said turning onto the street closer to the mansion. "They still fucking niggas in groups of threes in the back though?"

"Yeah, but they don't always enforce the rules. Sometimes it be four niggas at a time." He coughed. "But you know how that is."

"Hold up, you don't have that shit, do you?"

"Fuck you talking about, nigga?"

Derrick frowned. "You coughing on the phone and shit."

"That's cause I'm smoking this trash you brought me. I'm gonna have to start dealing with other dudes because this shits weak."

Derrick laughed. "Yeah, aight, I hear you."

"So, for real, you coming over later? Because that chick Zika been asking about you again." He paused. "And I'm tired of faking like I haven't talked to you."

"Tell her I'll get up with her when it's our time." To be honest, Derrick wasn't a cheater. He didn't have it in him.

"What the fuck, nigga? She bad as fuck!"

"I'm serious. There's a season for everything and I have to make sure it's right." He pulled into the driveway. "I'ma hit you back though."

"Later."

When the call ended, he walked into his house and was immediately greeted by Shay, holding her hands on her hips. Her braids were yanked up in a ponytail on the top of her head and she looked so pretty.

Out of all of her expressions, he preferred her mad face best.

"What's wrong with you?" He grinned, believing this was about her friend. "Because I don't have time for this shit tonight."

Actually, he did have time. He planned every minute.

She smacked him. "I'm sick of your shit, Derrick!"

He laughed. "Oh yeah, what I do this time?"

"You ate my fucking sandwich! You knew I was gonna eat that shit tonight since don't nobody cook around here no more. And you did it out of spite too. Because I fucked you in the alley and left your ass there."

It was one thing to get smacked due to fake fucking her friend, and a whole different thing to get smacked for eating a ham sandwich. "Hold up, you just hit me because I ate your food? As much as I feed your ass around here?"

She waved a hand in his face. "Fuck all that shit. I'm sick of you." She paused. "If I get something for me, I want it here when its time."

"You sound so fucking stupid."

"Yeah, whatever," she walked away before stopping and turning back around. "Oh, and Sandra told me what you did. You so dumb."

So, she did know?

And the worst part about it was that she didn't seem to care. The ham sandwich was obviously way more important.

Derrick followed her toward their bedroom. "So, you knew about that whore and you hit me about eating your food?"

"Derrick, I'm not tripping off that dumb shit with Sandra. I'm still gonna have my friends whether you want me to or not."

Not if he had anything to do about it.

He was so heated he snatched her by the arm. "Are you fucking around on me? Because somebody this lax definitely got something else going on."

She faced him. "Did you find my father?"

"I hate when you skip the subject! And Banks is not your father. I keep telling you that shit."

"Answer me!"

"Listen, I done already told you Banks is dead. Now if you—."

"Until you find him, I will never look at you the same."

"What does that mean?"

"We over." She stormed away. "I'm moving out!"

CHAPTER ELEVEN

Mason was driving down the road with Blaire in his passenger seat, feeling like a G. It took everything in his power not to tell her about the past, and yet a part of him, the part that he was ashamed to admit, liked what he was experiencing.

After all, Blaire was everything he wanted Banks to be. Beautiful, smart and above all, feminine. And at the same time under the surface sat Banks' real personality. The part that even while dressed as a female, was still connected to his life as a man, husband and father.

"...I don't know what got into Todd." She said. "One minute we were about to eat dinner and the next minute he snapped. It was like he had been holding back and suddenly realized he didn't feel like faking anymore."

"Wow." Mason shook his head. "You should've went the fuck off on that boy. Disrespecting and wasting your time. Had I known he was gonna go out like a bitch, I wouldn't have let him go on my date."

She giggled. "You shouldn't have." She looked at him and then out the window. "But, uh, anyway, I felt sorry for him in a lot of ways."

"Wait, what?"

"I know what you're thinking but, he seemed so desperate. He probably thought of that moment repeatedly and when he finally got it, things didn't go as planned. It's kinda sad you know?"

He did know and could sympathize a tad bit now that she put it that way. It was the story of he and Banks' relationship.

"Imagine waiting forever to get something, and have it so close, and still not know what to do." She continued.

Mason leaned deeper into his seat. He felt the same way. He wanted Banks to be Blaire. He wanted them to have their moment. And now that they did, he didn't know what to say.

The right thing to do was to tell Blaire who she really was. But what did that mean for their newfound connection? The way he saw it, did Gina break any major rules other than lying by not telling Banks of the past? After all, Blaire was born female. Not male. So technically, who she was now was closer to her core than anything they shared in the past.

Truce – A War Saga

"So, I've been talking all day." She turned her body to face him. She was so fucking pretty. "Enough about me. Tell me about you."

Mason shrugged. "I'm boring."

"I like boring."

He chuckled. "You saying that now, but I don't think things will be the same once I start rapping your head up."

"The last time I saw you, things didn't go the way I hoped."

Mason's head leaned back. "Wait, you had hopes?"

"To be honest, yes. What you did for Todd was sweet and I kind of wanted you to, you know, be different. Live up to that persona. But when you showed up you presented a different face and...I don't know..."

"I fucked up." He paused. "You don't have to clean it up, Blaire. Seriously. The way I acted is not really me. Well, not me all the time anyway. I had a friend who was really close to me once. And he, he always told me that sometimes I need to take it easy. To think before I act. He always told me that sometimes I moved too fast. But my heart be in the right place. Always."

"I believe you."

By T. Styles

He nodded and exhaled. "So, to answer your question, about who I really am, I'm a businessman."

"What kind of business?"

"Drugs."

Her eyes widened. "Wait, what you mean? Pharmaceuticals?"

Mason looked at her and could tell the truth would send her running in the opposite direction. Maybe forever. It wasn't like they didn't cut and move big bricks together. She didn't know about that shit.

So, he needed to change routes a bit. "Yes. Drugs to help with mental health issues and shit."

She nodded and sighed in what he thought was relief. "I figured as much."

"You sound relieved."

"Oh, no, I just, I don't know, something about you..." She took a deep breath and looked at him a bit longer. "Something about you I like."

A bit harder now.

Under her full focus, Mason stumbled. His breath rate increased, and his thoughts swirled. What if she recognized him? What if she didn't like what she saw? What if he reminded her of all the stupid shit he used to do?

Besides, when she was Banks, they stayed beefing about one thing or another.

But they loved each other too.

"Do you know me, Mason?"

"What...what..."

"I'm going to tell you something I never told anybody before. Well, other than my grandmother who is a wonderful person and everything but—."

"Wonderful huh?" He glared.

"Yeah, but she, I think, I think maybe she's lying to me."

"I need more, Blaire."

"I don't remember anything about my life beyond two years ago. At all. I don't remember who I am. I don't remember where I come from and I don't remember what I know. And every morning I wake up I feel like a fake."

"Nothing about you is fake."

"You're kind, but it doesn't change how I feel. And when you look at me...when I'm around you, I feel like maybe you know me more than I know myself." She sighed. "So, do you know me?"

"Hold up...I know this nigga not crazy." Mason said looking out of his rearview mirror at a car that he feared was following him for a mile.

By T. Styles

She looked back and saw the vehicle with the tinted windows too. "What's going on?"

Mason pulled over. "Nothing."

"Why do I—."

"Give me one second." He reached into his glove compartment and removed a loaded .45. When the car behind him, pulled up and flashed his camera, Mason realized it was the detective Jersey hired.

The driver sped off.

Mason was so enveloped in anger, that he didn't realize that Blaire was watching everything with a disapproving gaze. Taking a deep breath, he put the gun back. "Listen, I'm sorry about that shit. This—."

"Stop." She looked at the glove compartment and back at him. "Take me to my car."

"I will, I just…"

Fuck. He thought to himself.

"I don't know what you have going on. And I realize that we don't know each other well. But I'm a very wealthy woman and you're making me extremely uncomfortable. Now if this is some kidnap attempt, I—."

"Kidnap?" His eyes widened. "I would never—."

"To my car, Mason. Please."

After having dropped Blaire off, and speeding home, Mason parked his car in his driveway and pushed out of the vehicle, leaving the car door swinging open.

He was fighting, fucking, mad.

Storming through the house, he rushed up to Jersey who just put her daughter down in her room. Dragging her by the elbow, he led her into the hallway aggressively, slamming her against the wall.

"Fuck is wrong with you!" She landed a blow into the center of his chest.

"I thought I told you I didn't need no fucking detective!" He yelled, pointing in her face. Fingernail scratching her nose.

She glared. "I don't give a fuck what you need, my nigga! The fact that you don't seem to be looking for Banks and Howard, makes me not trust you. So, I'm taking matters into my own hands."

"By having me followed?" He beat his chest once.

By T. Styles

"Yes! You aren't trustworthy!"

"So now you think I killed my son and best friend? Is that what you saying?"

"I'm saying you're acting highly suspect. When we should be working as a team, Mason. I mean what the fuck. I'm asking for your help."

"You know what, I don't need all this shit." He was about to leave and chill at the apartment he bought for Joey. In the hopes that he could talk to Blaire on the phone, and she would be receptive enough to at least hear him mix up a fresh batch of lies.

"Who was the woman in your car?"

Mason paused with his back in her direction.

"Who was she, Mason?" Jersey grinned. "And does Dasher know about that bitch? Because the way she grilled me a few days ago, I'm sure she doesn't."

He turned around slowly. "Don't fuck with me."

"And if I do, what the fuck are you going to do?" She moved closer. "Because I'm not scared of you anymore."

"And that's your first problem." He pointed in her face. "It could be your last one too."

"Oh really?"

"If you think time changed me, you don't know me as good as you should, Jersey. And I'm warning you to be smarter. Before you end up hurt."

"Warning me huh?" She laughed. "We'll see about that. Because I won't give up until I find out where my son and Banks are. Period, Pooh."

"I let you stay here, because you pushed my homie's kid out that rusty pussy of yours. I let you stay here, because you the mother of my kids. But if you keep fucking with me, you can go back to that big ass empty house that Banks gifted you and get the fuck out my crib."

She giggled, walked in the back and grabbed her daughter. The baby's head was dangling like a loose titty because she was sleep. "You don't have to threaten me but once. But understand this..." she pointed at him. "This ain't over for me. I'm gonna find out what you hiding." She stormed out; the baby's head dangerously close to hitting the door.

The moment she left his phone rang. "Who is this?"

"You don't know me, but you're in danger. And your family too."

Inside her elegant bedroom, Blaire was pulling the covers up over her body, when the door opened, and Walid strutted inside.

"Mama, we gotta talk."

She was irritated with the broken language but after hearing her own self call a boardroom full of people niggas, she gave him a pass. "Yes, honey, is something wrong?"

"Mama, do you have to let people touch you if you don't like 'em?"

Her eyes widened in shock. "Touch you? Of course not!"

"Okay."

"Son..." She paused. "Is someone bothering you? At school?" She lowered her eyes. "Is it Carl?"

"No. Carl is fine."

She didn't like the man, but the kid was allowed to have an opinion. "Then what is it?" She rubbed his head lightly and gave him her undivided attention.

"Great-grandmother keeps touching me. And I want her to stop. And she won't."

"Touching you like what?"

"Like hugs and stuff. She likes kisses too. But I hate her lipstick."

Blaire sighed. She was fully aware that he wasn't a Gina fan, and at the same time she didn't know why. She was certain her grandmother loved her son. She could see it in the way she took care of them when she was learning to walk. But Walid wasn't feeling her whatsoever.

"Walid, what is it about your grandmother that bothers you?"

"Nothing, I just want her to leave me alone."

"Okay, let's do this. Does she hurt you?"

He shook his head no.

"Does she talk mean to you?"

"Not really. I mean, I don't care much. Just don't like her touching me."

"Then how about we do this, the next time she wants a hug, just hug her as hard as you can so that she knows you care. And then tell her, you want to go."

"Okay," he pouted, as if it were the worst thing in the world. Because to him, it *was* the worst thing in the world.

By T. Styles

"Give me a kiss." She laughed softly. "But only if you want to. I don't—." The phone rang and she looked over at it. "Honey, I have to take this. I'll tuck you in, in a second."

He nodded, kissed her on the cheek and hopped off the bed before walking out with the weight of the baby world on his shoulders.

She answered the call. "Hello."

"So, I wanted to ask you an important question." Mason said.

She shook her head and smiled. "What?"

"Do you use your hair care products, or are you just promoting the brand? Because I always wondered that about CEO's."

She laughed softly. "I use everything in my line."

"Oh, because I have to tell you, it's definitely working."

She shook her head. "What do you know about hair care?"

"Not much. I don't have any daughters so, you know, I'm just out here observing. That way I can stay informed in case I do. You know what I mean?"

"Mason, you called for a reason. So, what can I help you with?"

"Which hair care product would you recommend for me?"

She laughed and hated herself for it because she was supposed to be mad. But he was just so fucking charismatic. "I'm busy. I gotta go tuck my son in."

"Listen…" He breathed deeply. "Before you go, I, I just wanted to say that what happened in the car, with the gun and all, is not representative of the man I am. I'm a licensed gun carrier. And if you give me another chance, I'll make things right. I'll do right by you too." He paused. "I promise."

Officer Logan was checking the innards of his 1976 Mustang Cobra 2, when his wife brought out a cold beer. He enjoyed fixing up the car he'd come to love as a hobby. It was a bad ride and he knew it too. Got many compliments every time he pulled it out the garage.

His white face was covered in oil when he swiped at it to wipe off sweat.

"Thirsty?" She asked giving him a wide tooth grin. She was a thick young chocolate thang, which he couldn't keep his hands off.

Grabbing a handful of her meaty ass cheeks he said, "You already—."

BOOM!

Before he could finish his sentence, a bullet pierced the flesh of his forehead as he toppled to the ground. Blood splatters covered the silver and black ride as Mason and three of his men rushed up to the man's wife, who was frozen in fear.

Taking the beer from her hand he said, "This was a bad man who was going to kill me and my family." A deep sip. "And it don't matter if you know it but it's true. He killed a lot of people, even my connect from back in the day."

She trembled in place.

"Now you don't know me. And when I'm gone you better forget my face too. And for that ounce of respect, I will leave you and your son alive." He took another sip. "But if you get the notion to remember the features of my face and decide to share those features with a sketch artist at the Baltimore homicide division, I want you to be certain, that my people will come back to finish the job. And trust me, witness protection won't be able to hide your pretty face. Nod if we're clear?"

With wide eyes and tears rolling down her face, she nodded slowly.

He nodded back and bopped toward the van waiting on the curb. Looking back once he said, "Damn, you fine."

She ran into the house, screaming all the way.

CHAPTER TWELVE

Spacey and Minnesota were in amazing moods after having heard from Walid, and it was tough to conceal the fact that with a little attention, they may be able to use his help to get out of the garret.

But they had to be careful.

"Okay, so this is what we're going to do, we are going to be easy going with him." Spacey said softly. "You know, big brother and big sister like. That way he won't get afraid."

She giggled. "But we are his big brother and big sister."

"Ya'll are. But I'm not blood related."

They smiled at one another.

"Maybe we should have him try to unlock the door." She sighed. "You know, instead of beating around the bush. Because if this is our last chance, I don't want to mess it up."

"Now who's being pushy?"

"I'm serious, Spacey. Ever since he showed up at the door with that cookie dough I, I don't know, I have real hope."

Spacey stared at her for a minute. "So, all those times before the cookie dough you didn't have hope? Because that wasn't what you told me."

She pointed at him. "Never said I didn't have hope."

"Then what are you saying?"

She walked across the room and flopped on her bed. "At first I thought we were going to have to work on the maid and butler. Maybe even overpower them while pretending to be weak. But with Walid..." She shrugged. "I don't know, freedom seems closer with him involved. I mean, don't you feel the same way?"

He grinned. "Yeah." He nodded repeatedly. "Like, the fact that he is able to come up here with no problem. I feel lifted."

"Now what did you tell him when he came back the last time? I want to make sure we good."

"Okay, you were in the bathroom changing your—."

"Stop bringing up my period, Spacey." She rolled her eyes. "I already know you can't forget it."

He laughed. "Like I was saying. You were in the bathroom changing and he came back with another block of cookie dough. I told him he can't tell anybody he spoke to me."

By T. Styles

She nodded. "Okay, then what else?"

"I asked him how he was doing. He said fine. And then I asked, I asked about his father and he said he didn't have one."

Minnesota looked down. "You don't think..."

"What?"

"That Pops is...dead?"

Spacey sighed. "I been thought he was dead remember?"

"Do you think, that Gina, maybe, I don't know, is holding him hostage or something? Like in some weirder place in the house?"

"I really can't call it. Maybe we should—."

Keys rattled in the door.

As if they were caught stealing, both Spacey and Minnesota jumped up and stood next to the window. The door opened across the way, and the serving tray was pushed inside by the maid, with the butler closely behind.

On top of the tray was one plate, and the siblings looked at each other.

"Minnesota Petit, come with me." The maid said firmly.

"Wait...what's going on?" Spacey asked.

"Your meal is there." She pointed at it as if it were poison. "And we are taking Minnesota with us."

"No, the fuck you not either!" He snapped. "Not unless you tell me what's going on first."

All of the plans for them to act submissive, quickly went out the window. Because taking Minnesota was out of the question. He was the one who always left, never really telling of the things done to him behind Gina's closed door.

What if creepy things happened to her too?

"Are you coming with us or not?" The maid asked.

Minnesota looked at her brother. "It's okay."

"I'm not feeling this." He said with his eyes and his whole heart. "Please don't go with them."

"It's all good."

"You don't even know what's up, Minnesota."

"She'll be here." The maid said. "In the house. Safe."

"I'm not talking to you bitch!" He pointed at her.

"You better be easy!" The butler said. "Or else."

Minnesota grabbed Spacey's hand. "I'll be fine. I promise." She smiled. "Trust me." She hugged him hard and long.

By T. Styles

But he couldn't be calm. He didn't trust Gina. So, the moment she made it to the door, Spacey ran up to the butler in full attack mode. Instead of getting out on the man, he was met with a blow to the face.

"Spacey don't!"

It was too late. The butler pulled out a retractable baton and hit him over the head, before Minnesota was yanked out the door, kicking and screaming.

While Spacey lie in a puddle of his own blood.

CHAPTER THIRTEEN

Mason was sitting in his apartment looking at the view of Baltimore from the open window. He had been going back and forth about his next move, and whether he should call Blaire again, since his recent calls had gone unanswered, and at the same time he felt he didn't have much of a choice.

She was all he thought about.

She was and had always been his life.

Grabbing his cell phone, he decided to push off. It rung once, and he contemplated hanging up until he heard her voice. It was weird how much she sounded like Banks and at the same time, still possessed the well-rehearsed voice of femininity. Courtesy of Gina's extensive training he was certain.

"You feel like talking to me now?" He eyed the whiskey on the bar but paused on getting a glass.

"Ba..." he stopped himself from calling her real name. What was wrong with him? He couldn't even keep the names straight. At this rate, how was he going to keep Blaire straight too?

"Blaire, are you there?"

By T. Styles

"I'm here."

"Can I see you? Please?"

She sighed. "I don't know about that..."

He stood up and walked toward the window and leaned against the wall. "Please, I, I need to talk to you."

"Why?"

"Because, because you're right about some things. I'm not the man you think I am. In this moment." He paused. "So, can I see you so we can talk about it?"

"Are you going to tell me the truth this time?"

"I'm ready."

An hour later he was sitting in the park, waiting on Blaire to show up as they discussed. When she pulled up in her Range and the twins piled out, he grinned. The pride he felt in seeing his boys happy and healthy, couldn't be expressed into words.

They were the next generation.

Ace ran full steam ahead toward the playground, while Walid hung back a little. Almost as if guarding Blaire.

But when Walid saw Mason propped up on the bench, it was as if he were magnetized to him. Mason was stunned at his reaction. The boy was simply too young to remember him so why did he gravitate to him so easily? The time they shared was brief, before he and his brother were abruptly taken from his life.

He saw him once before after Gina kidnapped them, when Blaire didn't know, and he also appeared to recognize him then.

"Walid and Ace, slow down!" Blaire yelled.

She was wearing jeans and a long shirt that hid her figure. And as she walked, her long hair flew in the wind. Up until that moment he was confused on how he would handle their newly found connection. Would he tell her who she really was, or would he allow things to stay the way they were?

But looking at her face in the moment it was settled. He had no intentions on telling her about the past. Why would he? It wouldn't benefit the future. But Blaire, being the way she was now, would gratify all his needs.

He would make her his wife.

166   By T. Styles

And they would start anew.

He would break the world for a chance.

"You look beautiful," he said, as Ace hopped around and Walid sat closely next to him, as if examining each inch of his face.

"My son likes you." Blaire said, finding it very odd. "Almost a bit too much."

Mason tried to play it cool as he looked down at his handsome little face. "That's nice."

"No, you don't get it. He doesn't like anyone. Not even his great-grandmother unfortunately."

Mason found big humor with that fact. He couldn't stand the bitch either.

When he laughed, Walid laughed too.

Also a first.

The kid simply didn't smile.

"Well, I'm glad he likes me." He ruffled the boy's curly hair and Walid laid his head on his arm. "I like him too."

But Blaire was embarrassed. Seeing him take so hard to Mason put her off because she wasn't even sure if she would keep Mason in her life. "Walid, stop being weird."

"I'm not weird."

"I know, but you don't know him. So why lean on him?"

He sat up and glared.

"Now put your gloves on and go play. Remember, don't put your hands in your faces." As they put on their gloves, and walked to the playground, which was only five feet away, she sat next to Mason. "I have honestly never seen him like that."

"Well, maybe if he trusts me, you can too."

"That's a huge leap."

"I wouldn't say all that." He shrugged. "Children have a way of seeing the good in people where others judge the outside."

"I definitely don't judge by appearance."

"Meaning?"

She crossed her legs. But it was masculine style. Ankle to knee. "I mean, you look like trouble. You look like everything I should run away from. And yet I'm still here."

He nodded. "Wow."

"What?"

"Nothing." He shrugged. "Just didn't expect you to say all that I guess."

She giggled and the sound lit up his heart. "I've decided on the way over here, that for the rest of my life, I'm going to say what I'm feeling even if I feel stuffed."

By T. Styles

"Stuffed?"

"Yeah, it's like, sometimes I want to say certain things but I'm afraid that if I do, whoever I'm talking to may take it the wrong way. But I don't feel like having that burden anymore."

"Be careful. I say what I want all the time and it gets me in bad situations." He laughed.

"But I bet it's freeing too. To be able to say what you're feeling without taking it home and saying to yourself, *why didn't I say this*? Or *why didn't I say that*?"

Mason never thought about it that way. His way of living had always been the same, so he never thought about the freedom that came with speaking your mind. "I guess you're right."

She turned her body to face him, which again made Mason uneasy and lifted at the same time. How did she do that?

"So, tell me what you wanted me to know."

"I was wrong about my past."

"More, Mason."

He smiled. "I was a drug dealer. Narcotics."

She shook her head. "I knew it."

He frowned. "How?"

"Men with money move in the world the same." She paused. "At the same time, businessmen and drug dealers are different species. There's always an underlined stress factor with legal businessmen. They don't have full confidence that they will be able to continue the lifestyle they are accustomed to forever. If stocks crash. The market goes to hell. They die inside. But men in your line of work, they do what they want more often, knowing full well that when a million is lost, they'll quickly get another."

Mason was shocked she knew so much, since her memory was gone. He needed to know what caused such a powerful statement, but he had to be careful not to jog her memory which could ultimately end up with her wearing a rubber dick again.

"Met many drug dealers?" He joked.

She frowned and looked outward. "I...I don't know." She sighed and looked at him. "But, Mason, I can't be associated with crime. I'm sorry."

"I said my past." He continued. "I gave that up."

She smiled in relief. "Why?"

"Because it didn't suit me. It didn't suit what I wanted in the future. I'm into real estate now, using the money I made. Now I know that makes you uncomfortable, but I'm asking you not to judge a man based on the things he did when he wasn't smart enough to know the difference."

She looked at him. "I told you, you were trouble."

"But I won't ever bring trouble your way. Trust me."

"How can you be sure?"

"Because you are quickly becoming the most important thing in my life. And I keep the important things in my life safe at all times."

Her eyes widened. "And why would you make me your life?"

"You have always been, B."

She frowned. "What does that mean?"

He couldn't tell her he was speaking big facts, so he said, "I honestly believe I've been waiting on you. Doing my version of a prayer for you. And looking for you. And now that I have you, I don't want you to go." He paused. "And I'm going to show you."

"I can't have what happened the other night happen again. I can't be followed by strange men, Mason."

"I understand."

"I'm serious. I'm a private woman, with a company to run. The last thing I need is scandal. So, can you be sure that you'll never ruin my life?"

"I'm positive that I will kill to protect your peace. Always."

He had all intentions on living up to the promise too. Which is why he didn't let on when he saw the investigator taking pictures of them across the way.

But it didn't mean he would let it go either.

The investigator Jersey hired was on the phone at the park talking to his wife as he looked at the photos on his camera. He was excited that he had something substantial to show Jersey.

"Yep, this is gonna be good for us." He bragged going over the pictures. "I really think this is what she's been looking for. Part of it anyway. Still working on the Howard and Preach angle. She's gonna have to pay big money for these flicks."

By T. Styles

"Are you sure about this, honey? Because you said her husband was a dangerous man. Maybe you should let this case go. All money isn't good money, Tim."

"That's just it, I don't think they're together anymore. He's here with another woman who based on the pictures she gave me, looks an awful lot like the man she's looking for. It's all so strange and fascinating." He smiled in glee. "I mean, is it possible that they are the same person?"

"You don't think she's his twin do you?"

"I'm not sure." He paused. "Jersey didn't mention a twin." He yawned. "Now I have to go. I'll be home in time for dinner."

"You better. Because these late nights have been killing me."

He laughed as he prepared to upload the picture of Blaire, her kids and Mason wirelessly. "I know. But it's almost—."

Before he could finish speaking, the door was yanked open and he was snatched up by his shirt by Mason. "Didn't I warn you to stay the fuck away from me?" His eyes were cold and filled with hate.

"I'm sorry but—."

"Ain't no need for words. It's too late now." He grabbed a weapon from his hip and shot him in the face, leaving him slumped over his steering wheel as his wife cried bloody murder on the phone.

By T. Styles

CHAPTER FOURTEEN

Minnesota sat in a large bathtub with candles around the perimeter. The smell was thick with lavender essential oils in the tub. The purpose of the soft lighting was not romance but necessity. Because the place she was held didn't have lighting installed, and so it needed the draconian method to provide light.

When the door opened and the maid walked in, mostly with big attitude, Minnesota sheltered her breasts with her hands. "What is going on? Can you tell me why I'm in here?"

The maid tossed a pillow next to the tub, grabbed the soap from the black rack and a washcloth from the holder and snatched her wrist. Water was splashing everywhere. The soap smelled of chocolate and had the Strong Curls stamp embroidered on its side.

"What's going on?" Minnesota yelled, slapping the woman with her free wet hand. "I can clean myself."

The maid glared, smacked her hard in the face and grabbed the floating washcloth from the water to continue to clean her roughly. When Minnesota moved to fight back, the door opened revealing the butler.

She settled down and hid her breasts with her free arm.

"I wish you would tell me what's going on," she wept quietly. "For months you bring us food, but you never talk to me. You never talk to us. What did I do so bad to make you hate me?"

Silence.

The maid was not interested in talking. Her purpose was clear. To clean her up and get her prepared for an event. Which event was another question all together.

"Is my father alive at least?"

Her eyes fell on Minnesota's and she smiled evilly.

"What does that mean?" Minnesota asked, more nervous than ever.

The woman continued to clean both underarms, before standing up, and yanking Minnesota up to her feet as if she were a five-year-old. "Open your legs."

"I can clean my—."

She glared hard. "OPEN...YOUR...LEGS."

Minnesota looked at the butler and assumed the position. He didn't bother looking away. He wanted to see it all.

The woman continued roughly washing her vagina. It was painful and the most humiliating experience and it took everything in her power to keep the peace.

After the maid ensured that Minnesota was so clean her skin squeaked like a mouse, she stomped toward the sink, opened the cabinet and grabbed a jar of cream. "Moisturize your body and pull your hair in a ponytail. The cream works for your hair too. I'll be back shortly."

She stormed out the door.

Blaire pulled up to a gazebo in Reisterstown, Maryland. Most Marylanders didn't know about the location, but the locals did, and they cherished their little slice of heaven too.

When she made it to the gazebo, she saw a table decorated with fresh fruit, cheese, crackers and whisky. There was care and love put into the set up, and she couldn't help but smile. Most of all what caused her to feel a type of way, was Mason requesting to see her for the second time that day, since he had to abruptly cancel the park date.

His beard was neatly shaved, and he was wearing a soft black t-shirt with designer jeans. A small chain hung from his neck.

He was handsome but Blaire was beautiful per usual. She was dressed in soft black slacks, a red top and a designer fall jacket. She was doing her best to conceal her beauty by looking like a middle-aged serious woman, but she failed a little. "Mason, what is...what is all this about?"

"Have a seat."

She did. "Did you do this all for me?"

He poured two glasses of whiskey and sat next to her. Handing her a glass he said, "I've enjoyed our talks, but I think it's time to go deeper. Which is why I requested a second date."

She nodded. "For some reason, I wanted to see you again too."

"So, let's do this, let's talk with no judgement." He paused. "I really want to know how you feel.

By T. Styles

What you're thinking and if nothing else, what I can do to help."

She took a large sip and looked downward. "That's the first time anybody has ever really...really asked..." she sighed. "I was...never mind..."

He placed a hand on her leg. "Blaire, talk to me."

She sat her glass down. "I hate who I am. How I look."

Mason sat his glass down. Now would be a good time to let her know that the woman she was forced to be, was fighting the man he was born to be inside.

"I think you're a beautiful woman."

"Please don't, Mason. Beauty is so, so, superficial."

"Okay, well let's do this, is there anything specific you don't like about yourself?" He took a sip.

"That's just it. I can't pinpoint one thing and it has me, it has me wanting to...wanting to not exist. And I felt that way for months until I met you."

He smiled but released the grin when he realized it was a bit much and quite honestly, rude. "Okay, is it your hair?"

Blaire shook her head no.

"Is it your face?"

"No."

"Is it your body?"

Silence.

"Blaire, do you hate your body?"

"I think that's part of it."

What he wanted to know next was killing him inside. "Do you not like being a...a woman?"

Blaire looked at him. "I don't know that either."

Mason had to get her out of this funk before she searched too deeply and went full blown trans again. He wasn't willing to tell her who she really was, but he felt he could ease her pain. He touched the top of her jacket, that resembled a stylish woman's suit jacket and dropped his hand heavily.

Rising, he extended his hand. "Come with me."

"Where we going?"

"Trust the process."

By T. Styles

Minnesota was taken to a private bedroom that was set up as a dining room. A soft lamp provided light and she could see on top of the table were two plates that were covered on silver trays.

Would her father be joining her?

She hoped so.

Taking a seat at the table, she waited patiently. Five minutes later the door opened, and Gina's funky ass was pushed inside in her wheelchair, still connected to an oxygen tank.

When Minnesota first saw her, she almost didn't recognize the frail being, as she'd lost so much weight and aged greatly over the months. Being hateful had a tendency to age folks.

At the same time, it was definitely her. Her eyes were dark, cold and calculating.

The butler pushed her up to the table and stood by the door.

Gina removed her mask, her lips covered with orange lipstick. She smiled at Minnesota. "I can't get over how beautiful you are. You look so much like your grandmother it...it chills my soul."

"Th...thank you."

Gina nodded and removed a plate from the tray in front of her. It was a dish of fried chicken, mashed potatoes, green beans and a sweet buttered roll. She nodded at her. "Please eat. I know you're hungry."

She was.

Minnesota tore off the cover and begin to eat rapidly, using her hands and fingers mostly. She felt bad about Spacey being hungry and yet the tastes were exciting and invigorating on her tongue. While devouring her meal, she was thrust into a wheel of emotions.

"You know, your grandmother was a strong woman." She spooned mash potatoes between her thin lips. "So strong that at first, I thought we would have problems." She pointed at her with the spoon. "Well, I knew we would have problems actually. Angie always made it known that she would fight at all costs even if she could never win the war."

"Did she fight you?" She asked with her mouth opened.

"All the time. Strong women aren't meant to stay in the same house together for long. We are meant to be separated. To rule our own families. And your grandmother had such a hard time realizing that this was my house. And in my house, I am king."

Minnesota continued to eat. "Did things change?"

"It took some time, but after a while she found it easier to understand that either things would be my way, or they would be no way."

"Great-grandmother, I don't want to fight."

"I know, sweetheart. Although you remind me a lot of her. I didn't see it at first. But I see it now. You have the ability to manipulate men. And that worries me." She smiled. "I always had to pay and break down souls for mine."

"I just, I just wish I knew what you wanted from me. I wish I knew what to do, so that you wouldn't have to be so angry with us all the time."

"I'm not angry with you."

"So why do you keep us in the attic? Why is my brother given so little to eat, and I'm given a bit more?"

Gina placed her fork down and sat back in her chair. "What do you want in life, Minnesota?"

"To be free."

"Easy, one step at a time." She pointed at her. "Freedom is not good for all. Most don't know what to do with it anyway. Will you fight for it? Cry for it? Die for it?"

Minnesota sighed. "I want to be able to walk outside. To spend some time with Spacey. To be able to at least feel like I'm part of something else. I don't even know what's going on in the world and it's scary."

"Trust me. A lot has changed."

"Great-grandmother, I'm willing to do whatever I can to make things easier. To be a better person. I just need to know how."

Gina smiled. "I want you to be a part of this family."

"Okay, we can do that. And you won't have any problems from us. Because we—"

"I said *you*."

Minnesota glared. "What do you mean?"

"That boy upstairs is not of the Petit bloodline." She wiped her mouth. "Anyway, he had his chance."

Her heart thumped. "But my father raised him as—."

"He is of no relation. No more fitting to be amongst our people than an orphan or servant."

Minnesota looked at the butler who looked away. "I understand what you mean, I do. But I love him very much. I can't stand by and—."

"Here are your options as they are today. Be a part of my family or be a part of his. But trust me, Minnesota, you will have to choose. And soon too."

"What will happen to Spacey? Because I could never be able to sleep if—"

"Does it matter what happens to him?" She yelled.

"Yes, it does. Very much so."

Gina sighed. "If you decide to be a part of my family, if you decide to come home, he will be handled with the greatest of care. I understand how much you love that person. And so, I will care for him with kid gloves."

"So, he will be...killed?"

"No need to worry about such frivolous things."

Minnesota looked down. Suddenly she lost her appetite. "Where is my father, great-grandmother?"

"Your father is no longer."

Her heart thumped. "Meaning?"

"Meaning this...I have given you your options. You either stand with us, or you stand away from us. This offer is only available for the next 72 hours. I hope you choose family. For your sake."

Mason was waiting in front of a dressing room inside of a department store. When the door opened and Blaire exited, he smiled. She was wearing a baseball cap which still allowed her curly hair to fall over her shoulders, comfortable black sweatpants and a white t-shirt.

Most of all, she was wearing a smile.

"How you feel?" He asked. He was a little off balance, because in that moment, she resembled Banks. Definitely not a carbon copy. More like a younger Blakeslee who was trying too hard to be cool.

A look that he found cute.

After all, he'd dressed Blakeslee before when she was younger. But he also lost her when he did that too.

So, he had to be careful.

Nothing or nobody would stand in his way this time.

She shook her head. "I don't know what made you suggest this but for some reason I...I don't know." She smiled brighter. "I feel good."

CHAPTER FIFTEEN

After arguing for two hours, Dasher and Mason were sitting in the living room in his mansion. He hadn't been at that house all night, preferring instead to spend hours talking to Blaire on the phone in his apartment, so this was a shift in the wrong direction. And still, since she was pregnant, and his dick was legally responsible, he had intentions on trying to take it easy. Besides, he wasn't a mad man 24/7.

"...and in conclusion, I was going to leave you for good," she sniffled. "I know you don't believe me, but that's where I stood."

He nodded.

"But you would've like that wouldn't you?" She looked up at him.

"Dash, I don't want to fight with you. We been at this for hours and nothing changed."

"Then what do you want, Mason?"

"For you to realize that sometimes niggas move on."

"That quick though?" She threw her arms up. "It's been a little over a few years, and now all of a sudden I don't matter to you no more? Mason, if

By T. Styles

you are going to hurt me, if you are going to fuck me up, at least give it to me straight."

"Okay." He nodded. "I'm back with my ex."

She frowned. "What ex?"

"The one I told you about. The one I never got over."

"But I thought, I thought she was dead." She frowned.

"I did too." He sighed deeply. "But she isn't. And I can't, I can't have anything, or anybody get in the way of my plans. I need to see if we can put this thing together."

She glared. "It's Jersey isn't it?"

"Jersey?"

She jumped up. "Stop fucking around. Are you and Jersey back together or not? Was this all a game that you played with me? Huh? Did you ask me to move here so you could fuck her in my face?"

"Let me be clear, the last person I would get back with in this world is that stupid bitch."

"So why did you lie about the love of your life being dead?"

"I didn't lie. I just found out she was alive. Like I said. And I'm gonna take care of you and all. You can trust me because why else would Jersey's stupid ass still be living in my house if I didn't have the loyalty gene in my heart? But you have to understand something. There is nothing in the world that will stop me from being with the true love of my life. Nothing."

"Mason…"

He turned around and saw Jersey standing behind him.

"Did you…did you find Banks?" She trembled.

"Banks?" Dasher said to herself. "Is that who you were in love with?"

Jersey's eyes were wide open as she stared at him in the foyer. They were alone. "Mason, what did you mean by you finding the true love of your life?"

"I was just talking." He waved her off playfully. "And keep your voice down. I don't want to upset Dasher. She's been having real bad morning sickness and her belly—."

By T. Styles

"FUCK THAT STUPID BITCH!" She yelled. "Did you find my nigga or not?"

The hate he felt for the woman he swore at one time to protect was immense. "I keep telling you over and over again, if he was alive, I would've told you already. But you can't make me do shit I don't want to do."

"You're lying. I have known you forever, Mason." She wagged a finger like windshield wipers. "I have shared your dry ass bed too. Now she may be stupid and green, but that's not me anymore. Now do you know where he is or not?"

His nostrils flared. "I told you no."

She smiled. "My detective is close you know?"

"Close to what?"

"Everything. The truth."

He laughed. "That nigga ain't close to shit but his grave. That's fact."

A chill ran through her spine. "Why you think that? Because you know in the past you scared people off when they didn't do what you want? Do you think that will work again? I keep telling you my money is long thanks to Banks. So, whatever money you try to bribe him with to stop him from searching, I'll give him more."

"I said what I said."

"And I get all of that, but at the same time, you will understand that the meek woman you married is—."

"I don't give a fuck about no meek woman." He shoved her back just because he could. Mason was fully prepared to rock heads. "I don't even give a fuck about you!"

She laughed. "At least we know the feeling is mutual."

She smiled and walked out, leaving him in the foyer with Dasher, who had walked up behind him.

"Mason, what's going on?"

He dragged a hand down his face and sighed deeply.

"I should've stayed at my other crib. These bitches are killing me." He said under his breath.

CHAPTER SIXTEEN

Spacey sat alone, looking out of the window. Normally he preferred not to view the acres, because it made him sad. But over the past few hours he took to taking peace with the view, as it made him remember the things he took for granted in life.

It reminded him of how before the attic, he lived in a mansion, and had all the trappings of a young king, only to take his lifestyle for granted. It reminded him of when all of his family were together. When they were all alive, happy and carefree.

What he wouldn't give for an ounce of that time back.

Most of all he thought about his father, and how much he missed and loved him. He thought about his mother, and her desperate need for attention. How foolish he felt now that he craved the same thing but hated her for being weak.

Lastly, he thought about his wife. He wondered what she was doing, and how their baby was. He figured he'd be chunky and happy, and it fucked him up that he wasn't there for his first born because he walked into Gina's trap.

When the door opened and Spacey saw Minnesota walk inside, he exhaled in relief. He didn't know he was holding his breath until that moment.

Happy to see his face, Minnesota rushed over to him, her skin was bright and hydrated, and he figured she had a bath or shower. Her hair was also neat and up in a bun with not a strand out of place. She was wearing jeans and a white t-shirt that looked fresh out the package new.

She looked beautiful.

The moment the door closed she wrapped her arms around his thin waist. "I missed you so much."

She smelled of lavender and he pushed her away with two strong arms.

Was it jealousy?

Maybe.

She frowned. "Spacey, what's...what's wrong?"

He flopped on his bed and she sat on hers. "Nothing."

"So, why, why did you push me away?"

"No reason." He shrugged. "Just didn't feel like being touched is all."

"Spacey, I know, I know you were worried about me while I was gone. And I know you probably thought something would happen but—."

"Oh, I can see that you were fine." He said sarcastically. "Unlike me. So, basically I worried for nothing."

"That's not fair."

"Fair?" He glared. "They poisoned my food. I was in here shitting all night. And when I couldn't shit anymore, I vomited. But it's okay because you look good so who cares right?"

She got up and sat next to him. "I'm so sorry. I...I didn't know what their plan was and—."

"What *is* their plan? Huh?"

She looked down.

"Minnesota, what is their plan?"

"To break us apart." She whispered.

He stood up and walked toward the window, leaning against it he sighed. "I told you it was the plan all along. They were hoping I would die. But they didn't count on you keeping me alive with your food. So, when is the day?"

"What day?"

He looked at her. "The day I die?"

Tears rolled down her face. "They wanted me to choose to be with them. They wanted me to choose to, to live in the house. Downstairs. And eat their food. Wear their expensive clothes. But...but I had those things before at the Wales Estate, and they meant nothing. Kept saying that she needed to trust me with a secret. But first I had to give up you."

"I don't understand."

"Spacey, they wanted me to kill you myself."

"Wow."

"Spacey, I love you. And if they want to take me, to live with them, they'll have to take you too."

"BUT I DON'T LOVE YOU!" He yelled. "I DON'T EVEN LIKE YOU! I NEVER HAVE!"

She trembled. "Spacey, don't say that."

"It's true."

"No, it's not." She shook her head slowly from left to right. "You can't tell me you don't love me. I can see it in your eyes."

"Well its true. You ruined my life. You ruined all of our lives. You don't think I think about the fact that had you and Arlyndo not betrayed Pops, we would all be together and alive now?"

"Spacey..."

"Yes, we would be on Skull Island and out of the states. Yes, we would've been away from our

By T. Styles

friends and whatever lifestyle we had in America. But at least we would be together."

She looked down and shook her head slowly from left to right. "I'm so sorry."

"No, you aren't. You are selfish. And you will always be selfish."

Minnesota lied sideways on her bed as she cried hard and long. It was the type of cry that you can't come back from. The type of cry that rips you inside out. And at the same time, the pain she felt was the only thing that made her feel better. That brought on relief. Because at the end of the day, she knew he was right.

And then, as if a light flicked on, things made sense.

Slowly she sat up and looked at him. "I know what you're doing." She wiped her slimy nose with the back of her hand.

"What you talking about now?"

"I'm not leaving you."

"Just go! I don't want you in here with me! I don't want you around me."

She rushed up to him and laid her head on his chest. She could feel the pounding of his heart against her ear and knew that a man who's heart pumped that hard, couldn't help but love.

Wrapping her arms around him she said, "I know what you're trying to do. "She looked up at him. "And I'm not leaving you. Either they take us both. Or they kill us both. Makes no difference to me anymore."

He wrapped his arms around her and kissed her on top of the head.

One thing was certain, the young selfish Minnesota Wales was a thing of the past. And in its place was a queen.

CHAPTER SEVENTEEN

B laire sat in her office leaning back in her chair talking to John. The changes she implemented to portray all women of the rainbow in the marketing campaigns had done well, and sales increased by fifteen percent since the advertisements ran in both print and billboard format.

"You were right," he said. "I hate to admit when I'm wrong, but you were right." He continued. "The ad was very successful."

"You shouldn't hate to be wrong sometimes." She smiled. "It means you're human. And being wrong is where the magic begins."

"Meaning?"

"Well, if you always had the answers where's the fun? There would be no challenge. No purpose."

"You like fun, don't you?" He said, lowering his brow and licking his lips.

YUCK. She thought to herself.

"Not when it comes to my work. But always when it comes to results." When her phone rang, she hit the intercom button. "Yes, Javier?"

"You have a call from Mr. Arrogant."

She shook her head and smiled. "I'll take it." She picked up the handset while looking at John. "I'll talk to you later."

He nodded. "Of course." And walked out.

When she was alone, she leaned back. "Mr. Arrogant huh?"

"Well, I figured if I said Mr. Arrogant, you would definitely know who I was." He chuckled. "Since you named me and all. I go in for role play."

She shook her head. "I hear you talking."

"So, listen, I was hoping maybe we could get together. I wanted to spend some time with you the right way."

"What exactly does that mean?"

"For some reason, I had a flashback of how I came down your job. So, I wanted that first impression erased."

"I don't know that your first impression needs to be erased though."

"Why?"

"Because the first impression I had of you was donating a lot of money for a benefit that helped children. So, in my book the first was a good thing but if you want to change it—."

By T. Styles

"Nah, we can keep it like that." He laughed. "I was just thinking about the past that's all."

"You love talking about the past. *Stay in the present, nigga. It'll treat you much better.*"

SOMETHING HAPPENED.

A MEMORY!

At that moment, Blaire had a strange out of body experience when she believed she said those exact words. Many, many times. Which appeared to be all the more powerful saying them to him.

And then there was the word nigga that she used again.

Nigga.

Normally she didn't talk like that so why did it flow so effortlessly from her lips? Even sitting behind her desk, in boss mode, felt eerie.

"Blaire, are you okay?"

"Uh, yes...I...I don't know...I felt like I've said those exact words before."

"Oh, well, uh, did you want to do dinner or something?"

Blaire's door opened and Joanna walked inside. "Mason, I have to go. Can I call you back later?"

"Sure. Hit me when you can."

"May I come in?" Joanna asked, twiddling her fingers.

Blaire hung up the handset and smiled. "Since when do you ask?"

She smiled and sat down. "Never, but, well, this is different. I wanted to talk to you about Mason."

She frowned. "Okay, what about him?"

"I think he's a drug dealer."

Blaire sighed and sat back in her chair. "Why do you say that?"

"Well, I've been doing some research because—."

Her brow lowered. "Who authorized you to research him?"

"Since when do we need authorization to get into each other's business?" She laughed softly, before clearing her throat. "I recall you on many occasions getting into my business, and I never said a word. Now it's a problem?"

"Joanna, I didn't mean it like—."

"You are a wealthy woman. And you may want to be careful about the company you entertain."

Blaire glared. "What I do in my private time is my business, Joanna. And if you want to continue to be my friend, you will respect my position to its fullest." She said a bit louder.

"So, let me get this straight, you are going to continue to entertain a possible criminal?"

202   By T. Styles

"I think you should get out of my—."

"I'm in love with you." She said firmly. "Okay? And I...I don't want to see him take advantage of you. And...and...I know it's weird to hear. I promise I do, but it's the truth all the same."

Blaire sat back in her seat, as suddenly all was revealed. "You are my dearest friend. And you've gotten me through a lot."

Joanna shrugged. "So, I tell you I love you and that's all you can say?" Her pale face reddened. "What about me? What about us?"

"I'm sorry. But I don't feel the same about you. Never have. Never will."

She nodded and ran out.

"Joanna!"

Joanna was heated about being rejected as she stormed out of Strong Curls with high heels crushing into the pavement. And although she was sworn to secrecy, not to tell Gina Mason's name, she was willing to break all vows.

"Gina, this is Joanna."

"Yes, dear."

"I'm sorry to bother you. But we need to talk about Blaire."

"I'm listening."

"The man she was talking to, the one at the benefit, I found out his name."

"Joanna, dear, I'm not one for suspense. Who is it?"

"Mason. Mason Louisville."

Gina sighed. "Fuck! I don't know where Logan is these days. But I'll handle it. Thanks for letting me know."

CHAPTER EIGHTEEN

Jersey circled the floor of her mansion in the living room, with her cell phone in hand. It was purchased for her by Banks. She was on her twentieth call of the hour, after having put to sleep her daughter and her grandson and she was exhausted. But she was more concerned that she hadn't heard from her private detective.

After all, Mason made an eerie comment about him being in his grave.

Did he follow through?

She was just about to call him again when her doorbell rang. Immediately her heart pumped because as far as most knew, she was living with Mason. Her home always held an air of evil. After all, to her knowledge Banks had died there, and so she never felt safe.

Walking slowly toward the door, she was surprised to see Dasher sobbing on the other side.

"Dasher...what are you...what are you doing here?" She looked around from where she stood, out onto her property.

"I need to talk."

Jersey sighed. "Dasher, I don't have time for—."

"Please?"

A few minutes later they were in her living room, sitting on the sofa. "I know you don't like me, and I'm sorry to intrude. But I need your help."

"I never said I don't like you."

"Well that's how it feels." She looked down. "And I get it but—."

"The problem I had with you was related to Mason. He seems to forget his promises."

"Promises?"

"Mason is supposed to be helping me find our son and Banks. And when he gets around you, he gets stupid. And irresponsible. It's important for me that I find both of them. So, if you're in the middle of us fighting, I'm sorry."

She sniffled a few times although her tears had long since dried. "Can I ask you something?"

Jersey nodded yes.

"Is Mason, um, is he gay?"

Jersey laughed hard.

"What's funny?"

"I don't mean to laugh but if ever there was a straighter man on planet earth, Mason would be it."

206

"So why do I get the impression that he's in love with Banks?"

Jersey sat back. "So, he never told you?"

"Told me what?"

Jersey sighed. "Banks was born a woman."

Her eyes widened. "I...I don't understand what you...he...I saw him and he...it's...I don't..."

Jersey placed a hand on her thigh to calm her down. "I know it's shocking, but it's true. Banks was born female, and back then his name was Blakeslee."

"But he got you pregnant. And he—."

"There are ways to do many things when you're rich. And we are very wealthy people, Dasher."

"So, why would he love him if he's not gay? Because even with him being born a woman, everything else about him is masculine."

"They met as children, before Banks transitioned, and well, he still holds on to the hope that they could possibly be together. But I plan to stop all that shit."

"So, it's true, that he's alive?"

"I think so but I'm not sure. He lies so fucking much and I..." Jersey's phone rang, and she hopped up and answered. "Who is this?" She didn't recognize the number.

"Is this Jersey Louisville?" The frantic woman asked, crying hysterically.

"Yes, who is this?"

"I'm Amanda Luther and I need to see you! It's about my husband!"

Standing in her driveway, Jersey sat in front of the private investigator's frantic wife. She looked as if she hadn't slept in a few days, and her eyes were crusted with dry tears. Jersey was getting tired of the sobbing women that seemed to surround her lately.

Just too damn weak.

"I'm sorry to bother you but I..." she sniffled and wiped gel from her nose with her fingertips. "I didn't know who else to go to."

"Where is Tim? Is he okay?"

The woman looked down and slowly rose her head. "No. He's, he's dead."

By T. Styles

"What?" She placed a hand over her heart. "How did that happen?"

"Your husband killed him! That's how it happened!"

Jersey took one step back, after getting a healthy dose of the woman's violent tone. "First of all, I haven't been married to Mason in quite a while."

"But your last—."

"My last name has nothing to do with my connection with Mason. We are done. Been done." She took a deep breath. "Now I'm very sorry about your loss. And if you don't mind, I'd like to find more information on why he was killed. I don't suggest you tell the police about Mason though. Or you may suffer the same fate." She was about to walk into the house.

"Wait! I need to show you something!"

Jersey paused and turned around. "What?"

She dug into her pocket and removed a phone. "They didn't find his camera. I know the killer has it. But before he was murdered, he sent me something. And I want to, well, do you know this woman and her kids? I'm not sure but I think they tie into everything he wanted to show you."

Jersey looked at her and stepped closer. Gazing down at the phone, her knees buckled under her weight when she saw the video. She hit the ground.

"Ma'am, are you okay?"

She wasn't.

Instead, now, she was the one sobbing. Because after so much time, she had seen the twins she had given birth too, and the man she had fallen in love with all together. And they looked great. "When did he send you that video?"

"The night everything happened. We were talking on the phone when...when all of a sudden I heard his pleas."

"I need you to tell me everything you know. Now!"

Mason was walking out of the building of the apartment he rented when he saw Jersey approaching him with the quickness. "We need to

By T. Styles

talk." She was aggressive as fuck. Almost like a rattlesnake ready to attack.

"About what? I got some place to—."

"I saw Banks, Mason! I fucking saw him!" Her face was red, and tears ran down her cheeks.

He looked around from where they stood. The coast was clear. "Come with me."

"I want answers!"

"I will give them to you. Just come with me."

A few minutes later they were in his half-furnished apartment. The moment she saw the set up, she glared. As a bit of misplaced jealousy tackled her spirit. "I thought this was supposed to be for Joey. What are you doing posting up in here? I—."

"He's staying in Arizona. Says it's better for him there." He sighed. "Now what are you talking about you saw Banks?"

"I'm talking about your lies, Mason! And there ain't no need in you faking. I know he's alive. And I also know why you don't want him to change."

"Fuck does that mean? Of course, I knew where he was." He smiled. "I was going to tell your fine ass." He joked trying to touch her. He was fully prepared to dick her down if necessary.

She slapped away his hand. "Mason, cut the shit."

"For real. But I wanted to wait to make sure he could handle things first."

"Nah. You had no intentions on telling him. Because finally, after all this time, he's the woman you always wanted him to be. And a beautiful one at that!" She shook her head at how Banks was so pretty, he could slide into a woman or male with ease. "What you do? Pay to have his memory removed or something?"

"Shut up, Jersey."

"You shut up! I know you did something. Just like you mixed your sperm and ruined our pregnancy, by becoming Ace and Walid's father." She cried. "Did you have all of his memories of me erased? All of his memories of his children? Just so you could have him for yourself?"

"Shut up, Jersey!" He said a bit louder. "You sound stupid! That shit ain't even possible! I checked."

"No matter what you do, no matter what you try and say, I will always be in his life. Do you hear me? Always! And I will tell him who he really is even if you won't. If I can't have him, you won't either."

By T. Styles

Those were fighting words.

Before she could continue, Mason rushed up to her, wrapped a hand around her back and lunged a knife into it. There was no denying at the moment that the person he would kill the world for, was Banks Wales.

And that the mother of his children was, well, disposable.

"I'm sorry," he said, as he dropped her on the floor before rushing out the door.

CHAPTER NINETEEN

Mason was listening to *FYH* by *TGT* as he pulled up to the meeting place he and Blaire designated. When he saw her standing next to the waterfall, he rolled the window down and she smiled. It was like he was dating Banks' beautiful twin sister, and he felt tremendous pride.

"Waiting on someone?" He asked.

She grinned, rushed over to his car and slid inside. "Wow, that was quick. Thought I'd be out here for five more minutes." She focused on the music for a second. "Nice song too."

"Thank you."

She nodded. "You know, everybody wants me to stay away from you right?"

He shook his head and slid into traffic. "The story of my life." He turned the music down.

"If it's the story of your life, what does that say about you?" She leaned back. "I mean, if everybody you know says you're trouble, aren't you trouble?"

"I'm only trouble to those outside my circle."

"And am I in or out?"

"You know the answer to that already."

She giggled. "I want to ask you something."

By T. Styles

Since many questions had been sprung on him over the past few days, he grew nervous. "Okay, but before you ask do me a favor."

"Anything."

He loved the sound of that. "In the future, just ask. The lead up is terrible."

"Okay..." She paused. "Who is Jersey Louisville?"

His mouth opened and closed. Now that he thought about it, it was a good thing she warned him. "I don't know, I mean..."

"You do know, Mason. And I know you know. I even feel like I know that name. I just don't know why." She looked straight ahead as he approached a light.

"Well, uh, what happened?"

"I received a call from my secretary earlier today, that someone by the name of Jersey Louisville wanted to talk to me. And when I heard her name, it...it sent chills up my spine. Sort of like it did when I saw your face."

He nodded. Left leg shook rapidly. "Oh."

She sighed. "It scares me because everyone I meet; everyone I see appears to know more than I do."

"That can't be easy."

"It's not. And what I need is a friend. What I need is someone who is really there. Someone who won't lie, to help me sort all of this shit out."

He nodded. "Can we go somewhere private?"

"Where is somewhere?"

"I have a place."

"I don't know about this."

"You just said you wanted someone you can trust right?"

"I did but..."

"Well this is part of the trust process."

She sat back.

"Listen, this isn't about money, Blaire. Not to be arrogant but I'm good on that front. This isn't about me trying to hurt you either."

"I believe that."

"Why?"

"Because, when I look into your eyes, I feel like you're the only one in the world, who truly has my interest at heart. More than my grandmother. More than my employees and more than my friends." She briefly thought about Joanna.

His heart rocked. "So, if you believe that, then go with the flow. Go with me."

Minnesota and Spacey were on hand and knee, talking to Walid under the doorway. Since his first visit, he had become a regular fixture and they really enjoyed his company. He was intelligent, confident and more than all wise beyond his years. It was as if he'd been in the world before.

But best of all, Walid could keep a secret.

"So how old are you?" Spacey asked.

"I'm four years old."

"That's good," Minnesota said looking at spacey, letting him know with her eyes she was about to press him for more information. Something he forbade her to do earlier. "How is your daddy?"

"I don't have a daddy."

Spacey widened his eyes and tilted his head, essentially saying, "Now will you let it go?"

But she wouldn't.

"What about your mommy?"

"My mommy is nice."

Minnesota resituated on the floor. "Is she?"

"Yes. She gives me hugs. Kisses my belly and stuff like that. I don't like it as much as Ace does. But she's still a very nice woman."

Minnesota and Spacey couldn't help but laugh. "What's your mommy's name?" Spacey asked figuring Gina gave her a new mom.

"Blaire. My mommy's name is Blaire."

"You think that's Pops?" He asked, whispering in Minnesota's ear.

"I don't know." Suddenly Minnesota remembered the two women jogging behind the mansion. The taller light skinned one looked familiar, but she put that thought away. But now, considering how things turned, she wondered if it could be her father after all. "Walid..." Minnesota continued.

Silence.

"Walid, are you there?"

"What were you talking about just now?" The little boy asked. "I heard whispering. And I don't much like whispering."

They looked at one another, surprised he knew they were plotting behind a closed door. "Nothing, little man. We were just—."

"I don't like when people whisper about me. It makes me mad."

218   By T. Styles

Minnesota covered her mouth. "I'm sorry. I can—."

"I'm gone!" Suddenly they could hear his feet pitter pattering as he ran away.

After witnessing his level of intelligence on full display, they sat on the floor and leaned against the door, while looking at one another.

Spacey sighed. "I always knew he was deep but..."

"I know right?" She said. "He's...he's so in tuned it's scary."

"I feel sorry for whoever is on his wrong side when he gets older."

"When he gets older?" She repeated. "I feel sorry for them now."

Walid was walking toward the kitchen to get himself a cookie, when the butler walked up to him. "Where were you?"

"Nowhere." He glared up at him as if he were his same height.

The Butler looked at him long and hard and then grabbed his little hand. "Come with me."

"Get off, man!"

The Butler paused and let him go. "I'll stop holding you, but you must come now. Your great-grandmother wants you."

A few minutes later, they were in Gina's room which smelled of menthol, lavender and stale air. She was lying on her sofa, watching television. "You can leave, Carl. I want to talk to Walid alone."

Walid stood in the middle of the floor, with his arms behind his back. Baby general style.

Carl nodded and walked out. "I was looking for you. Your brother wanted to play hide and go seek, but he couldn't find you."

"I was busy."

She laughed. "You hate me don't you?"

Silence.

"If only you knew the lifestyle I saved you from. Then maybe, just maybe, you would come to appreciate your future. And you wouldn't be so fucking cynical."

Silence.

"Walid, are you going up high in the house? Where you aren't supposed to roam? Toward the attic?"

Silence.

"Walid, I don't want you upstairs anymore."

"But why?"

She glared. "Because I told you so. And when I tell you something, I want you to respect and obey my rules."

Silence.

"Do you understand?"

He nodded yes, more to get out of her room than anything else.

"Now come over here and give me a hug."

He shuffled his weight from one foot to the next. "No."

"Didn't your mother tell you never to deny me a hug? Didn't she give you clear instructions on how I'm to be treated?"

She was right. Blaire had given full instructions to hug her whenever asked. "Yes."

"Then get over here."

Slowly Walid walked up to her. When they were face to face, he climbed on the sofa. His hard shoes stabbing into her flesh, like her body had mountain cliffs, caused her to moan in pain as he made the rough trip up to her nose. When he reached the top, his belly was directly over her face as he hugged tight.

"Walid...stop..."

He wouldn't listen. Instead he gave her the biggest hug he could. A hug so strong, an elderly frail woman couldn't fight a young boy if she tried.

Even if she needed to breathe.

With his belly button directly over her nose, she couldn't pull for air, and she was getting weaker by the second. She tried to push away his weight, but it wasn't working. He hugged tighter, and tighter...and tighter.

And in the end, snuffed out her life.

When he was finished, he climbed down and looked at her. Her eyes were open, but she wasn't moving. Loving the silence, he smiled and placed his hands behind his back again.

Baby general style once more.

And the Butler, who had reentered quietly, stood in the doorway.

CHAPTER TWENTY

Shay was sitting in the backseat of a black Mercedes with Gordon, who just recently relocated to Maryland from New York. When she first met him, she wasn't interested in cheating on Derrick, but then she reconsidered since she was moving out. Something about his eyes called to her spirit, so she decided to take the dark ride.

Despite the possibility of being smacked in her face if Derrick ever found out.

But she could care less. Besides, her friend was dead and she felt Derrick did it, even though she didn't have proof.

In her entire life, she'd been under the protection of strong male role models. Of men who could unleash war to protect their own. And with her strongest ally, Banks, being 'supposedly dead', she felt misguided. And she needed direction. Fortunately for her, the thoroughbred from Brooklyn was more than willing to do the job.

"I can't believe you're single," he said, wiping her braids off her shoulder as she sat on his lap in the backseat of the car, looking directly into her eyes. "You're cute as fuck."

"Um, sir, I don't need you to tell me I'm cute."

He chuckled. "Fuck that mean?"

"For starters I'm well aware. What I need is someone who plans to ride for me. At all times and in all ways."

He nodded. "And why does a little thing like you need so much protection? Shouldn't you be getting your nails done with friends or—."

"You know what, you're starting to make me rethink."

He frowned. "Rethink what?"

She shrugged. "Everything. At best you sound weak and at worse you sound like a punk. So, you tell me, which one is it?"

He pushed her back a little, although she remained glued to his lap like cement. She was comfortable there. "Aye, mami, never come at me like—."

"I told you what I need. And if you in a position to give it to me, you can get as much of this good pussy as you can handle." She laughed to herself. "I don't even want your money because my adopted daddy took care of me a long time ago. So, are you with this shit or not? That's all I need to know."

He nodded. "If you need somebody to protect you, then—."

Before he could finish, Derrick opened the back door, yanked her out like money from an ATM and dipped inside of the Benz in fury. With the man's shirt under his grasp, he punched him repeatedly in the center of the face until he passed out.

Blood splattered everywhere.

Next he grabbed her by the arm, and dragged her to his truck, all while she had a smile on her face.

When he tossed her inside, she folded her arms tightly over her chest, while looking straight ahead. "What, Derrick?"

"WHAT DERRICK?" He repeated, with his nostrils flaring. "Am I tripping or were you just about to fuck dude in a car like a paid prostitute?"

"I don't know what you talking about."

"I'm tired of playing these fucking mental games. The world is going crazy right now. And this is when you choose to be disloyal?"

"Disloyal?" She yelled. "Are you fucking serious!"

"Yes, the fuck I am!"

"I don't want to be with you no more, Derrick. I don't want a fake ass relationship either. I want—
."

"I love you, Shay." He said under his breath. "Don't leave me, baby. Please."

"W...what?" She wiped her braids out of her face.

"I love you. And...and I don't want us fighting. I know I haven't been there for you and this need to find Banks but—."

"Wow, I never thought I would hear you apologize for abandoning me. Or saying you want me."

"I never said I abandoned you." He pointed her way.

"Did you kill my friend?"

"I swear I didn't." He raised a hand, American style. "I left her in the bushes where she belonged. But she was alive and breathing."

"Well somebody..." She squinted as she looked ahead. "Hold up, is that, ain't that Nasty Natty in that pink Range up there?"

He whipped his head in the direction she was looking. When he saw the woman perceived to be dead in the driver's seat, his jaw dropped. "Yeah, I think...I think it is."

"I told you that bitch was alive!"

He put the truck in drive and headed quickly in her direction. When Natty pulled up in an alley

226   By T. Styles

known for selling weed, he eased in behind her so she couldn't get out. The moment she saw their faces from her rearview mirror, she wiggled out of the front seat in an attempt to run on foot. Unfortunately for her, they had been looking for her forever. There was no way they would let her go and so, they caught up to her within seconds.

Out of breath she said, "Please don't hurt me!"

Shay rushed her and slammed her into her truck. "Where the fuck have you been?" She pointed in her face. "Huh? Where were you?"

"I was scared! I had to...I had to get away from everything and everybody."

"Bitch, scared for what?" She asked shoving her again.

"Gina, she, she was about to kill me!"

"Gina?" Shay frowned. "For what?"

"Wait, how much do you know?" Natty asked rotating her head from left to right as she eyed them both.

"Tell us what the fuck is going on, ugly bitch!" Shay continued although the girl was horribly cute. "Don't worry about all that other shit."

"Well, as you know Gina is Banks' grandmother. And she was going to have me killed to keep her secret. So, she sent her son Hercules out of the house to get me. But he had plans of his own and wanted me to stay alive. But, he told his mother he murdered me but just dumped my car in a river instead."

"So that's why they found your Benz." Derrick said to himself.

She nodded. "I guess."

"So why didn't he kill you?" Shay asked. "You ain't that cute."

She was.

Natty couldn't stand her but she would have to let that one go. "He never said. But I have a feeling he wanted something to hold over his mother's head. I also know they beefing. He gets drunks sometimes when he comes over, to talk about everything under the sun."

"Wait, you fucking a white man?" She asked.

"I'll fuck anybody to stay alive. Plus he fine."

"I bet you will." Shay said looking at Derrick and then back at Natty, while remembering their brief sexual encounter.

"Listen, these are powerful people." Natty warned. "You have to be careful."

"We dangerous ass niggas too." Derrick said stepping closer.

"True." Shay nodded.

"I know. But he had my life in his hands at that moment. All I was doing was dropping Minnesota and Spacey off at Gina's mansion, when the next thing I know he was coming out to kill me."

"Wait, you know who has Minnie and Spacey?" She asked. "You know where Gina lives too?"

"Yeah. And when I dropped them off, they were alive."

"Aye, Natty, I think you best be telling us everything you know." Derrick said. "Now!"

CHAPTER TWENTY-ONE

Mason opened the door inside of the luxury hotel suite as Blaire cautiously entered. She knew he had ulterior motives but the moment she stepped foot across the threshold, she was blown away at how elegant he made the environment.

Outside of the decorations, there were candles, soft music playing, a platter of fresh cheese, fruit and crackers on the table. These refreshments, were coupled with expensive whiskey prepared for her pleasure. The windows were also opened, revealing a stunning view of downtown Baltimore at night, which was somewhat more subdued than it had been before 'the virus'.

"You really like cheese, don't you?" She asked looking at the table.

He laughed. "Nah, I just wanted something to hold you over."

"Hold me over for what?" She turned toward him. "What is this about, Mason? Talk to me."

"I wanted us to spend some time together." He closed the door and walked over to the bar. "So, wine or whiskey?"

"Whiskey."

By T. Styles

Mason was already grabbing the liquor bottle. Out of her view he smiled, knowing that in the past, he and Banks shared the drink on a regular.

After pouring their glasses, he offered her a seat on the sofa, where they could get an even better view of the city.

She took the glass and sat next to him, although not as close as he would have desired.

Taking a sip, she said, "This really is beautiful."

He nodded. "I've seen better."

She shook her head. "I know you aren't going to try and flood me with compliments just so you can..." her words floated away.

"Just so I can what, Blaire?"

"You said you wanted to talk, Mason. I'm here. Let's talk. What's going on?"

He took a larger sip and in unison, she did the same. Placing his cup on the floor he said, "I'm in love with you."

She frowned. "What...how is that even...possible?"

"I've seen you before, in the past, and I always wanted to express how I felt. I always wanted you to know that even if you didn't realize it, that someone was in the world, actively wanting nothing but your safety, peace and happiness."

"Why do I feel like I should be scared?"

He frowned. "I don't know, baby. Please don't be scared of me. Ever."

"It sounds like you were stalking me for starters."

"Never. I would never stalk a person I care about. Although I was always there if you ever needed me. And would come in a hurry even if you didn't call."

She sat her glass down. "Mason, I..."

"Can you honestly say that when you look at me, you don't feel *something*? You don't feel that special connection that can't be placed into words? Because I feel it with you, B. I swear I do."

She took the moment to gaze into his eyes. To examine the features of his face. For some reason she knew every mole, every freckle and every line, as if it were her own reflection. As if she'd taken them to memory so many times, it was second nature.

Had she?

The answer was yes.

"I *do* feel something."

"Then why can't we begin to work on who we are meant to be? Which if you ask me, is together."

She got up and walked toward the window. "Because I don't know what that means. Every day I wake up feeling like I'm in, like, um...like..."

He walked over to her. "Talk to me."

"Like I'm in somebody else's body." She looked down. "Who's body is this, Mason? Because it isn't mine. I know it."

Silence.

"I'm confused, Mason. I'm scared. And even that motion contradicts what I feel inside. It's like, like, in another time and place I was strong and so I can't reconcile being this fucking weak. And nothing anyone says brings me relief." She lowered her head.

"Try me."

"But how?"

Suddenly he kissed her. She started to fight back, but she lost the round. It was as if her lips were magnetized against his, and she pushed a little harder into him.

Closer.

Mason, on the other hand, felt faint.

You have to understand, this was the moment he had waited on all his adult life, and he felt anxious. If he wasn't careful though, it would teeter along the lines of full-blown rape.

Wrapping his arms around her body, he squeezed and pulled her closer to his frame. His swag was out the window. Aggressive. And not in line with romance.

"Mason...slow..." she begged.

"I'm...I'm sorry...did I hurt you?" He released her and looked her over.

"No, I just...I haven't...I don't know...what I'm doing."

He nodded. "You're right." He took a deep breath. "You don't know. Let me show you. Come with me." He extended his hand. "There's no need to rush. We'll go as slow as you like."

Tender Love by the *Force MD's* played in the background as Blaire lie face up on the bed, with Mason over top of her. She was wearing navy blue panties, and a matching tankini top that kept her shape intact, while also concealing the breasts prosthetics that looked just like her body.

By T. Styles

Mason wore a black beater, and silk boxers. The gold in his chain sparkling.

"Are you okay?" He asked softly looking down at her.

She shook her head. "This feels wrong..."

He looked away, fearing she would say those words. "Oh..."

"...and at the same time, right." She continued. "How is that possible?"

He lowered his head and kissed her softly, careful not to move too quickly like he had a moment ago. Careful not to appear so, young and animalistic. With a few more moves, her panties were a thing of the past.

She smelled fresh.

Untouched.

Like fresh rain falling on a field.

Wrapping her arms around his body, Mason felt like he was floating while being seduced by her touch. It was hard to describe the feeling of wanting something so badly, and finally being so close to that moment. And yet, he didn't need words. All he had to do was go with the flow. To cherish each second, knowing that it was possible that it could be their last.

"You feel right." She whispered. "This feels right."

He smiled, kissed her neck and released himself from his boxers. He was stiff. Big. And warm. He slowly gained entry into the door of her body. She was tight, after all, she hadn't touched a man since they had sex as teenagers.

She was his first.

She was his next.

On the contrary, she had lived her life as a man. She had a wife, two if you count Jersey. But Mason was always a part of the picture.

Mason was her first love.

Always.

"Oh...this feels...so...um...is it supposed to hurt?"

"Are you okay, Ba...Blaire?" He whispered in her ear.

She nodded. "I think so."

"I'll be easier."

And so, he did, allowing himself to move like quicksand. Slowly, even slower, until he sunk so deeply, her body warmed up and provided the oil necessary for him to stroke with ease. It took everything in his power not to bust. Because he needed this moment to last.

236   By T. Styles

A lifetime if God was willing.

When he raised his head from her neck, she kissed him again, slipping her tongue in and out of his mouth. He may have thought he was taking advantage of her memory loss before, but in that moment, it was obvious that she wanted him just as much as he wanted her.

On a deeper level.

That couldn't be described.

The only question was, did Banks want him as a man also but was afraid to push off?

Did they *fall* to titles, like who was masculine and who was feminine, instead of choosing to *fall* for love instead?

When her kisses got too sweet, he knew there would be no way he could hold back.

"Fuckkkkkk..." he said, begging his body not to betray the moment by reaching an orgasm too early.

"Mason, I'm, my body...I don't know what I'm feeling..."

"I'm here, baby," he whispered. "I got you." He held her tighter.

In and out he continued to stroke until her juices covered his dick, dampening the alter beneath them. At one point they disconnected from the sexual sensation and connected more with the rhythm of their breath.

They were in sync. As if they were making music that only they could hear. Wrapped inside the warmth of each other's arms, they fell deeper to a place that no one else was allowed.

"Mason, I...I'm..."

"You're about to cum, B. Just let it go. I fucking love you. I've always loved you. Thank you for choosing me."

He continued to pump in and out, until she yelled his name. "Masonnnnnnnnnnn, I love you."

"I love you too."

She sang the words he had been looking for all his life.

And just like that, he came inside of her, leaving every drop in her waiting body.

When they were done, he slipped out slowly as they faced one another in bed. "I want to tell you something else now."

She smiled and nodded up and down. Out of breath. In ecstasy and relaxed. "Okay."

"We were married."

Her eyebrows rose and suddenly she laughed. "Yeah right."

"I'm serious. You were my wife. I was your husband. And Ace and Walid are my sons."

She examined his face for a lie but couldn't detect one in the moment. Sitting up in the bed she said, "You're, you're being dishonest."

"Those boys are my sons, I swear it."

She yanked the sheet, covered her body and crawled out of bed. "That can't be true. If...if it were true then...then..."

"Look at me." He jumped out of bed, using only his hand to cover his dick. "Look at my face. Can you honestly say it's a lie? You know me, Blaire. And we had a fucking life together I swear!"

"So, all of this was just to fuck with my head?"

"No! I wanted you to see me. I wanted you to *feel* me. So that you would know it was real. I mean think about it, Blaire. You said it yourself that you loved me just now. You loved me because you were my wife, and I was your husband, before you suffered a brain injury."

"It was cancer."

"No, it wasn't! You had a tumor and it was removed. We tried to do it on our end and fucked up. And your grandmother stole you in the middle of the night. I'll give her that. She did save your life."

"But my grandmother never told me about you. She told me my husband died. And I—."

"I'm your fucking husband! I'm right here! And your grandmother is a fucking liar." He stepped closer. "Now I know all of this is too much. But take my D.N.A. I want you to. And I promise, you'll have all the answers you need to know. Those boys are my flesh and blood, and you were my wife. And I've come to take you home."

By T. Styles

CHAPTER TWENTY-TWO

The next morning, Mason pulled up in front of Blaire's mansion and parked before taking a deep breath. Looking over at her he said, "How are you? I know you had a rough night but...I want to check in."

She sighed, leaned back and looked at the mansion. "It feels like everything I know was a lie." She turned her head toward him. "Is everything I know a lie, Mason? Are you lying too? Because if I find out you are, nothing will be the same. And I will never, ever, talk to you again."

"I'm going to help you sort all of this out. I promise. But it starts with the twins."

"I'm gonna need time, Mason." She sighed. "But at the same time, I saw how Walid responded to you. He's a kid, it's true, but he's also wise and..."

"I am his father."

"I don't want to be here." She was so overwhelmed. "I don't want to live with grandmother if what you're saying is true."

"Then you can be with me." He breathed heavily. He was so close to sealing the deal. "We can live as we lived before. As husband and wife again. I can make a life for us I promise. I met you as a kid. We are childhood sweethearts. Even got the pictures to prove it." He was delirious with wanting her in his life.

"Wow...."

"Just trust me, Blaire. You've waited too long for what feels right. The time is now. And it starts with the DNA test."

She could tell by how adamant he was that he was telling the truth. And it scared her to the core.

She nodded. "I have to talk to my grandmother and—."

He lowered his brow. "She's going to say awful things about me. She's going to lie. But you can't believe her because she would have been honest about my sons. She would have been honest about me. Your grandmother's vicious ways were the reason I had to lie about who I was when I first met you. She did everything in her power to stop us from being together. But she couldn't stop me from finding you. You have no idea how many nights I drove down this street, counting every tree, because I knew it would bring me closer to this house. Closer to you and I finally being reunited. And I don't want anything to fuck that up. Don't let her push us further back, Blaire. Please."

"When I woke up, I couldn't walk. I couldn't do a lot of things. And that woman in there nursed me back to health. She gave me a purpose and it's not as easy as you think to just...to..." Suddenly her words trailed off.

"What is it?"

"Who is Bethany Wales?" Her memories were flooding back in waves, causing her headaches.

Oh shit.

He touched her hand. "She's from your past. And I'll explain everything when you're ready. Okay?"

She took a deep breath and nodded.

She wanted to know right away about everything she forgot, and at the same time she didn't have the energy in the moment. "I'll call you later, Mason."

He tried to kiss her, but she exited the car.

His mind was reeling, and he hoped he hadn't pushed too far. But his agenda was clear. To build the family he wanted with the person he adored. Turning off the property, he was shocked when he saw Derrick, Shay and what looked like Natty in the car approaching Gina's mansion. Blocking their position, he exited the car quickly and yanked the driver's door open.

They all piled out.

"What are you doing in this neighborhood?" Mason asked with clenched fists, ready to rock foreheads if they were going to approach Banks.

"What *you* doing here, Pops?" Derrick looked at his hands and his eyes. He looked like a madman ready to risk it all.

Mason relaxed a little. "Listen, I don't know what you about to do, but I can't let you fuck shit up."

"You know where my father is don't you?" Shay asked, with her arms crossed over her chest. "You might as well tell us. We on the way in now. Natty's ass done already said she thinks Minnesota and Spacey are still in Gina's house."

He glared and backed up. "Fuck you talking about in the house?"

Natty spent the next five minutes telling him everything he needed to know. When she was done, he had a more involved plan in play. The details entailed saving Spacey and Minnesota, and giving Blaire a little of her history to suit his purposes when she met all them niggas at once.

Finally living happily ever after with the woman he loved.

And to think, he wasn't even a romantic type nigga.

Blaire walked into the kitchen to make some coffee and then check on the children, only to see the Butler and Walid eating cereal at the table.

Shocked at the scene, she smiled. "Where's, where's Ace?" She asked.

"He's still asleep." The Butler responded coolly. "Walid and I got hungry and decided to grab a bite. You want something?"

She shook her head. "Nah." She sighed. "How is grandmother?"

The Butler looked at Walid and then his cereal. "She's sleep I believe. She said earlier this morning that she didn't want to be disturbed. The nurse is coming later."

She nodded and poured herself a cup of coffee.

"Mama, can you come with me?"

She smiled. "Sure, son. Where are we..."

Before she could finish her sentence, she was led through the large house, into the elevator and further up the stairs. When they stopped, they were standing in front of a door. "What is it, Walid? Grandmother doesn't like us up here."

"I can't open the door." He pointed.

She frowned. "Honey, this is grandmother's room. Where she keeps her private things."

"But I need to get inside."

"I don't have a key, Walid."

"Please, Mama. Try."

"Walid, is that you?" A voice said softly within the room. "If it is can you bring more cookies? We're hungry."

Blaire's heart pounded in her chest, as she recognized the voices immediately. She knew she heard something before but they told her she was crazy. Her head was spinning because she was also confused.

What was a person doing in there?

She was just about to kick the door down when the maid rushed behind her. "You are not allowed to be in there."

Blaire glanced down and snatched the necklace which held a key from her neck. "Excuse me, you aren't supposed to—."

246   By T. Styles

Blaire shoved her back and opened the door.

When she tried to approach Walid pointed at her and said, "Stay away from my mommy!"

Spacey and Minnesota appeared in the doorway.

Shocked to see the transformation their father held, but relieved he was alive, Spacey and Minnesota rushed up to her and wrapped their arms around her body.

The nurse who came by to see about Gina from time to time, rushed up to them. "Please come! It's Gina! She's dead!"

In a hurry, Mason pulled back up to the Petit Estate, ready to wage war if Minnesota and Spacey were behind those walls. But the moment he reached the house, Spacey and Minnesota came running outside to get free.

Yelling, screaming, and going crazy.

It was Shay who spotted Banks first within the car. "It's my daddy!" Shay yelled. "He's alive! He's fucking alive! I told you so!"

"Hold up, why the fuck does he look female?" Derrick frowned.

"He looks the fuck good to me," Natty shrugged.

Mason whipped his head around and looked at everyone in the backseat. "Listen, do not tell Banks who he is right now!" He warned.

"But why?" Shay glared. "He looks like a woman!"

"Because I fucking told you so! We will tell him together, when the time is right. Now wait here."

Mason piled out of the car just as Spacey and Minnesota rushed into his arms. They were hysterical when they saw his face. Because they knew he meant love.

"Uncle Mason, thank you, fucking thank you!" Spacey said thinking he was responsible for their freedom.

Minnesota simply wept, as Mason maintained a hold of them both, while he looked at Blaire whose eyes were wide with shock as she stood in front of the door.

Who are all of these people?

"Go get in the car," Mason whispered to them.

By T. Styles

"But what about, P—." Before Spacey could say Pops, Mason grabbed his head and whispered in his ear. "He doesn't know who he is. Don't tell him right now. It'll make things worse."

Spacey looked at them both and they slowly walked over to the car and embraced the others.

Walking up to Blaire he said, "Where were they? We thought they were dead?"

"Mason, what's going on? Who are those people?"

"Are you okay?" He asked trying to control the situation.

She wasn't. She was rattled beyond belief. "No...he kept calling me Pops. Why?"

"I will explain everything. I just have to get them some help. They are probably hysterical too." He stepped closer. "Are you okay though, baby? I don't want to leave you like this."

"My grandmother is dead." She tried to conceal her pain. "She was found in her bed this morning."

"I'm so sorry, Blaire."

He wasn't but he had to say something right?

As he spoke to her, Minnesota, Spacey, Shay, Derrick and Natty, all stood on the side of the car, staring in their direction. The look of shock on their faces having seen Banks' drastic transformation.

Blinking a few times, Blaire looked at Mason. "Can you take the twins with you? I have to take care of things here."

"Anything for you. Anything at all."

EPILOGUE

Mason was in his kitchen within his mansion, on the phone pacing erratically. He was talking to the Remover Man, Fido. He was responsible for getting rid of corpses for the Louisville's but in Mason's case, something went wrong.

"Well it doesn't make sense," Mason whispered. "I told you to pick her body up from the apartment. She was in the living room. And all of a sudden she's gone?"

"Boss, I went like you asked. I swear. And she wasn't there."

Mason felt sick to the stomach. It was crazy how one moment he was on top of the world with Banks back in his life, and the next he was horrified. Not only because of the fact that Jersey may have survived, but also that she could return and ruin it all.

"Keep looking. I don't—."

"Pops, everybody's here." Derrick said entering the kitchen.

"Okay."

Mason ended the call and walked into the living room where Minnesota, Spacey, Derrick and Shay were gathered. Joey was on Facetime; which Shay was holding in her hand. He was so excited that Minnesota and Spacey had returned, that he wore a huge smile on his face on the screen. He was also elated about the news that Banks was alive. Christmas had come early for the young man.

Standing in front of them all, Mason took a deep breath. "Are the kids sleep, Shay?"

"Yeah, Ace and Walid are dosing off. And the nannies are with Patrick and Blakeslee now."

"Mom still ain't called though," Derrick added, slightly concerned.

He nodded. "First off how are you two doing now?" He looked at Spacey and Minnesota who were standing close to each other. Her stomach was a bit round, and she looked a few months pregnant. "I can't imagine what you must've been through, being in a room that long with your sister."

"We aren't blood related." Spacey said.

Everyone looked at one another.

Since when was that a factor?

"What does that mean?" Mason asked.

"It means we good over here," Minnesota responded, looking at Spacey and then back at Mason.

"And you, Spacey? How are you?"

"I'm okay, I guess." He crossed his arms over his chest, not liking the attention. "I just wanna know what's the plan with Pops?"

Mason was mad uneasy with the duo. "Are you two comfortable? At the new house? Because you're welcome to stay here."

"We like it there. It's home." Minnesota nodded.

He nodded, still in detective mode. "So Spacey, when are you going back to your wife?"

"What is this about?" Minnesota yelled with an attitude.

"Well, the maid said you two are still sleeping in the same room. Isn't it time you split up now?"

"We fine," Spacey said with a lowered brow. "Now what's up?"

Mason took a deep breath and tried to leave the weird subject alone, figuring them being connected at the hip, was due to living together nonstop for years. "I know we talked about a lot over the past few days, but I need to go a little further." He continued looking at all of them.

"What is it, Unc?" Joey asked from the video screen.

"Like I said earlier, we can't let Banks know about his past right now. I will be working closely with him, to make sure—."

"But he's wearing dresses and shit," Shay interrupted.

"You act like that's off from who he was born to be." Derrick said. "I mean, he *is* a woman."

"Well, I don't like him like that." Shay continued.

"Me either if I'm being honest," Spacey said. "It ain't natural."

Mason frowned. "He's a woman," he said firmly. "Who dresses as a woman. What could be more natural than that?"

Everyone had a comment, making the room loud.

"QUIET!" Mason yelled. When the room grew silent, he said, "Now I know everyone wants things back to the way they used to be. And we will get there, but for now, we need to keep the peace, for his own good."

They all nodded, although some weren't feeling it one bit.

"Did you find ma?" Derrick asked. "Because she ain't been answering my calls."

"She ain't been answering mine either." Mason responded as if he didn't put a blade in her back himself. "Don't worry though, she'll show up soon."

Mason, Derrick, Shay, Minnesota and Spacey sat in the back of the church, while Blaire sat in the front with the Petit family for Gina's funeral. They hired an experienced nanny for Patrick and Blakeslee, since no one had seen or heard from Jersey in over a week.

Ace and Walid were also present, sitting next to the Petit family in the front row.

"Uncle Mason, I don't like Pops like that one bit." Spacey whispered. "I mean look at him. He's still wearing a dress. Don't you—."

"Are you that selfish that you can't see that she's having a hard time? Huh? I will tell Blaire about her past when the time is right. We just talked about this shit."

"His name is Banks, not Blaire." Spacey said.

"I hate to admit it, but I like her the way she is." Minnesota said.

Mason smiled.

He did too.

"Why you like that shit?" Shay shrugged. "Because I don't. I mean look how he walking. It's barely feminine. He trying too hard to pass if you ask me."

"Well nobody cares what you like." She responded. "Because contrary to what you believe, you're not blood."

"And neither is Spacey, but you treat him the same. Even sleeping in the room with him and everything. Or is it the same bed?"

Everyone looked away.

"Let's just everybody calm down," Mason whispered. They sure were making excess noise in the back row. "I will tell her about her past. I will tell her about you all too. But only when she has time to understand without being stressed."

Just at that moment Walid left the Petit family in the front, and walked toward the back, to sit next to Mason. Confused, the entire church looked to see where the rich baby mogul roamed.

Bringing more attention to the Wales and Louisville clan in the process.

They looked guilty as sin in the back row.

Because they were guilty as sin in the back row.

When he took his seat next to his daddy, Mason kissed him on the top of his curly head. "Yeah, everything will fall into place." Mason said, looking at his squad. "But everything will fall my way first."

Blaire was just about to go to the limousine when Hercules and Aaron Petit approached her after the service. Mason and his crew were still in the church, waiting for the crowd to break so that the nosey people who wondered where they came from, would not follow them home or ask a bunch of questions.

"Listen, today has been rough, but we need to talk." Hercules said.

"About what?" Blaire asked.

"Strong Curls. And what you intend on doing with the business." Aaron responded.

She shrugged. "Now is not the time, but even if it was, you don't have a claim. It was willed to me. Plus, I ran everything with grandmother before she died and—."

"You are a Petit, that much is true, but don't make me destroy you."

"Hold up, is that a threat?" She asked stepping closer to him, shocking him to his core at her aggressiveness.

He smiled, as a hint of who she really was, came shining through.

"Is everything okay?" Mason asked walking up to them.

Blaire looked at Mason, back at Hercules and walked away. Except this time the walk was different. Steadier and firmer into the earth.

More like, well, Banks Wales.

When she left Mason asked the Petit brothers, "Is there a problem?"

"Not really." Hercules shrugged.

Mason recognized the voice immediately. "Hold up, you called me about Logan."

"I did."

"For that I say thank you. But is there a problem with Blaire?"

"Other than I see you are intentionally not telling him who he really is. Which is shocking since we thought you were a friend."

"Never question my fucking loyalty."

"We won't." Aaron said. "As long as you don't question our stake in the business."

Hercules smiled. "We don't have any problem with keeping your secret. For all we care, you two can run off into the sunset. Just as long as you get us what's due. I hope we have a deal. I'll be in contact."

They walked away just before Mason's phone rang. When he looked down and saw Dasher's number, he rolled his eyes. He hadn't heard from her in days, and to be honest, he welcomed her absence. "What?"

"I told you to make space for me in your life, didn't I?"

Here goes this dumb bitch. "Now is not the—."

"Oh, it's the right time," a familiar voice replaced Dasher's, causing Mason's heart to rock. He looked around and at the exact same time saw Derrick walking out the church with Shay.

Mason walked a few feet away, to get more distance from his son. "How did you, I mean, how did you—."

"Survive?" Jersey laughed. "You mean after you assumed the Remover Man would get rid of my body because you left me on the floor in an apartment to die?" She giggled. "Well it didn't work, sir."

"Jersey, if I wanted you dead you would be dead. I left you alive on purpose."

She laughed so loud he removed the phone from his ear for a second. "I always knew you were a liar." She paused. "But thank God Dasher showed up when she did. And thank God I'm alive to tell my son what kind of man his father really is. And I believe Blaire, whose number I also have, may want to know the truth too. Don't you think?"

Just then Mason heard Derrick's phone ring. When he removed it from his pocket he smiled widely. Pointing at the screen he said, "Hey, Pops, it's ma! She's back!"

Mason's eyes widened in fear. "Jersey, please don't do this." He whispered. "I don't want a war with you. We family."

Instead of speaking to Jersey, Dasher returned to the line. "Nah, baby daddy. It's too late to call *truce.*"

By T. Styles

The Cartel Publications Order Form

www.thecartelpublications.com

Inmates **ONLY** receive novels for $10.00 per book **PLUS** shipping fee **PER BOOK**.
(Mail Order **MUST** come from inmate directly to receive discount)

Shyt List 1	_____	$15.00
Shyt List 2	_____	$15.00
Shyt List 3	_____	$15.00
Shyt List 4	_____	$15.00
Shyt List 5	_____	$15.00
Shyt List 6	_____	$15.00
Pitbulls In A Skirt	_____	$15.00
Pitbulls In A Skirt 2	_____	$15.00
Pitbulls In A Skirt 3	_____	$15.00
Pitbulls In A Skirt 4	_____	$15.00
Pitbulls In A Skirt 5	_____	$15.00
Victoria's Secret	_____	$15.00
Poison 1	_____	$15.00
Poison 2	_____	$15.00
Hell Razor Honeys	_____	$15.00
Hell Razor Honeys 2	_____	$15.00
A Hustler's Son	_____	$15.00
A Hustler's Son 2	_____	$15.00
Black and Ugly	_____	$15.00
Black and Ugly As Ever	_____	$15.00
Ms Wayne & The Queens of DC **(LGBT)**	_____	$15.00
Black And The Ugliest	_____	$15.00
Year Of The Crackmom	_____	$15.00
Deadheads	_____	$15.00
The Face That Launched A Thousand Bullets	_____	$15.00
The Unusual Suspects	_____	$15.00
Paid In Blood	_____	$15.00
Raunchy	_____	$15.00
Raunchy 2	_____	$15.00
Raunchy 3	_____	$15.00
Mad Maxxx (4th Book Raunchy Series)	_____	$15.00
Quita's Dayscare Center	_____	$15.00
Quita's Dayscare Center 2	_____	$15.00
Pretty Kings	_____	$15.00
Pretty Kings 2	_____	$15.00
Pretty Kings 3	_____	$15.00
Pretty Kings 4	_____	$15.00
Silence Of The Nine	_____	$15.00

Silence Of The Nine 2	_____	$15.00
Silence Of The Nine 3	_____	$15.00
Prison Throne	_____	$15.00
Drunk & Hot Girls	_____	$15.00
Hersband Material **(LGBT)**	_____	$15.00
The End: How To Write A	_____	$15.00
Bestselling Novel In 30 Days (Non-Fiction Guide)		
Upscale Kittens	_____	$15.00
Wake & Bake Boys	_____	$15.00
Young & Dumb	_____	$15.00
Young & Dumb 2: Vyce's Getback	_____	$15.00
Tranny 911 **(LGBT)**	_____	$15.00
Tranny 911: Dixie's Rise **(LGBT)**	_____	$15.00
First Comes Love, Then Comes Murder	_____	$15.00
Luxury Tax	_____	$15.00
The Lying King	_____	$15.00
Crazy Kind Of Love	_____	$15.00
Goon	_____	$15.00
And They Call Me God	_____	$15.00
The Ungrateful Bastards	_____	$15.00
Lipstick Dom **(LGBT)**	_____	$15.00
A School of Dolls **(LGBT)**	_____	$15.00
Hoetic Justice	_____	$15.00
KALI: Raunchy Relived	_____	$15.00
(5th Book in Raunchy Series)		
Skeezers	_____	$15.00
Skeezers 2	_____	$15.00
You Kissed Me, Now I Own You	_____	$15.00
Nefarious	_____	$15.00
Redbone 3: The Rise of The Fold	_____	$15.00
The Fold (4th Redbone Book)	_____	$15.00
Clown Niggas	_____	$15.00
The One You Shouldn't Trust	_____	$15.00
The WHORE The Wind		
Blew My Way	_____	$15.00
She Brings The Worst Kind	_____	$15.00
The House That Crack Built	_____	$15.00
The House That Crack Built 2	_____	$15.00
The House That Crack Built 3	_____	$15.00
The House That Crack Built 4	_____	$15.00
Level Up **(LGBT)**	_____	$15.00
Villains: It's Savage Season	_____	$15.00
Gay For My Bae	_____	$15.00
War	_____	$15.00
War 2: All Hell Breaks Loose	_____	$15.00
War 3: The Land Of The Lou's	_____	$15.00
War 4: Skull Island	_____	$15.00
War 5: Karma	_____	$15.00
War 6: Envy	_____	$15.00
War 7: Pink Cotton	_____	$15.00
Madjesty vs. Jayden (Novella)	_____	$8.99
You Left Me No Choice	_____	$15.00
Truce – A War Saga	_____	$15.00

(**Redbone 1 & 2** are **NOT** Cartel Publications novels and if **ordered** the cost is **FULL** price of $15.00 **each**. **No Exceptions**.)

264   By T. Styles

Please add **$5.00** for shipping and handling fees for up to **(2) BOOKS PER ORDER.** (INMATES INCLUDED) (See next page for details)

The Cartel Publications * P.O. BOX 486 OWINGS MILLS MD 21117

Name: _____

Address: _____

City/State: _____

Contact/Email: _____

Please allow 8-10 BUSINESS days Before shipping.

PLEASE NOTE DUE TO COVID-19 SOME ORDERS MAY TAKE UP TO 3 WEEKS BEFORE THEY SHIP

The Cartel Publications is NOT responsible for Prison Orders rejected!

NO RETURNS and NO REFUNDS
NO PERSONAL CHECKS ACCEPTED
STAMPS NO LONGER ACCEPTED

9 781948 373159